A prolific and ⎡...⎤
more than twe⎡...⎤
Teeny Wonderful, The Vandarian Incident and *Spin Out*.
Before becoming a full-time writer in 1985, Martyn was a
teacher in elementary and junior high schools in both On-
tario and Alberta.

Martyn's wide interests range from anthropology to the
Arctic, and his hobbies include collecting comic books and
growing older. He lives in Edmonton, Alberta.

Don't Worry About Me, I'm Just Crazy

Also by Martyn Godfrey

Don't Worry About Me, I'm Just Crazy

MARTYN GODFREY

Stoddart

A GEMINI BOOK

First published in 1992 by
Stoddart Publishing Co. Limited
34 Lesmill Road
Toronto, Canada
M3B 2T6

Canadian Cataloguing in Publication Data

Godfrey, Martyn
Don't worry about me, I'm just crazy

ISBN 0-7736-7364-4

I. Title

PS8563.034D6 1992   jC813'.54   C92-093280-0
PZ7.G6Do 1992

Typesetting: Tony Gordon Ltd.
Cover Design: Brant Cowie/ArtPlus
Cover Illustration: Paul McCusker

Printed and bound in Canada

Contents

1

A THREE-DAY HOLIDAY?

I was daydreaming about Rachel Parsons. Cute, five freckles on her nose, curly brown hair, best-looking girl in eighth grade at Maid of the Mist Middle School in Niagara Falls, New York. That Rachel Parsons. The one I was afraid to talk to.

I was wondering what it would be like if we were shipwrecked on a deserted, tropical island.

Just Rachel and me.

Alone.

Together.

Wearing leaves.

"Robert Fowler!" Mr. Miller shouted. "Do you have any idea what I am talking about?"

I left Rachel on the imaginary beach and focused on my science teacher. He was staring at me through his thick glasses, and tapping his pen on the overhead projector.

Tap-tap-tap.

"Any idea at all?" he asked. His forehead was flushed pink with anger.

"Of course, sir," I lied. "I find this unit really interesting. Science is my favorite subject."

He studied me for a few moments. "Please tell me what today's lesson is about, then."

I glanced at the overhead screen and quickly read the list of vocab words Mr. Miller had written. I vaguely remembered him talking about farmers and crops. But there was nothing on the screen about corn or wheat. So I chose the last word on the list.

"You were telling us about monoculture," I said.

Mr. Miller arched his eyebrows in surprise. I'd guessed right. "Hmmm," he mumbled to himself.

I noticed my best friend, Paul Lawson, watching me. He looked worried. Course, Paul always looked worried nowadays.

Mr. Miller tapped his pen faster. "Please repeat the definition of monoculture."

"Repeat the definition?"

"Is there an echo in here?" he said sarcastically.

"Monoculture," I began. "Well, it's . . . it's what you told us."

"And what exactly did I tell you?"

Tap-tap-tap-tap-tap-tap.

"It's . . ." What the heck was *monoculture*? The word was definitely familiar.

Tap-tap-tap-tap-tap-tap.

Then I got the flash. Of course, it wasn't a crop; it was a disease. "It's that sickness you get from kissing. That's it."

TAP!

A couple of kids chuckled. Mr. Miller silenced them with a snap of his fingers.

"I think you can catch monoculture by drinking from the same glass as somebody else," I continued. "You don't have to kiss . . ."

"Enough!" Mr. Miller yelled, so loud half the class jumped. "I am tired of your behavior in science class."

"What's wrong with my behavior, sir?" I asked in my polite voice.

He tilted his head and glanced at the ceiling as if he was looking for divine help. Then he spoke slowly, like he was explaining a complicated science formula. "Robert Fowler, I am tired of your fooling around during the experiments. I am tired of the way you fail to pay attention to my lessons. I am tired of the number of times you forget your textbook. I am tired of your silly sense of humor."

"Oh, that stuff," I said.

"Yes, *that stuff*." His words dripped anger. "I want you to report to the office."

"The office? But Mr. Miller, I'll get a week's detention for sure."

I might even get suspended, I thought. The last thing I needed was Mom screaming at me even more.

Last week, when I accidently smoked out the kitchen in Home Ec, Mrs. Druchek, the assistant principal, said I was one step away from a forced, three-day holiday.

She overreacted. The pan of fudge I was supposed to be watching didn't catch on fire or anything. It just overheated a little, making this black smoke, which made everybody feel sick. But it wasn't *that* bad. I think Lynette Koble was faking when she threw up. And it only took an hour to get the smoke out of the room.

"Report to Mrs. Druchek's office immediately," Mr. Miller ordered.

"I don't deserve this . . ." I began, but stopped when I saw Mr. Miller's forehead change from pink to red.

As I gathered my books and trudged out the door, I noticed the expression on Paul's face. He looked like I was about to go over the Falls in a barrel. "Good luck, Roob," he whispered.

* * *

"Good afternoon, Roob." Mrs. Lawson, the school secretary, looked up from her computer as I walked into the office. "Mr. Miller has already called down to say you would be arriving. Mrs. Druchek will see you in a minute."

Mrs. Lawson is Paul's mom. She once joked that I'm in trouble so often she gets to see me more at school than she sees Paul at home. She's also one of the only adults who uses my nickname, Roob.

Back in fifth grade, I mailed a coupon to join the fan club of my favorite comic book character, Super Bad Dude. When my membership card arrived, they'd spelled my name, *Roobert* Fowler. Paul thought it was so funny he started calling me Roob.

I sighed and sat in one of the office chairs.

"Is it serious?" Mrs. Lawson asked.

I shrugged. "I don't know, Mrs. L. I sure hope I don't get booted out. Mom will bird-dance on my face if that happens."

She chuckled. "Somehow I can't picture your mother doing that."

"We've been having a rough time lately," I confessed.

"Well, I don't think you'll get suspended," Mrs. Lawson said, trying to reassure me. "Paul tells me your father is going to visit soon."

"That's right," I answered. "Any day now."

The last time I spoke to Dad, four weeks ago, he said he'd be in Niagara Falls by the end of April. Today was May 3.

"Has he written any new books?"

"Probably. He writes a couple of *Boy Scout Buddies* and *Baby-Watchers Gang* books a year. Then there's the

Junior Romance Novels for Boys. I can't keep up with them."

"Say hello to him for me when he visits."

"You bet. Mrs. L, since we have a minute, can I talk to you about something? Something about Paul?"

She looked suddenly anxious.

"Please don't tell Paul I said this, okay?" I began. "But I'm a little worried about him. We've been friends for a long time. And he's always been kind of intense, you know what I mean? But lately, he's been majorly uptight. We don't seem to be having any fun together anymore. He's always studying."

"Paul realizes the importance of getting good grades," she said.

"He's always been head of the class," I pointed out. "But now, if he doesn't get an A+ on every assignment, he gets completely bummed out."

"He sets high standards for himself. I don't mean to be rude, but maybe it wouldn't hurt if you followed his example."

"That's not rude," I told her. "My mom figures if I was half as good as Paul, I'd be perfect."

Mrs. Lawson shifted in her chair. She seemed edgy, really uncomfortable.

"When he isn't studying, he's training for the stupid track team," I went on.

"Running is something our family is good at," Mrs. Lawson said. "You know Mr. Lawson was a champion runner in high school. He'd like to see Paul achieve the same. Maybe even better."

"That's just it, Mrs. L," I said. "I think it would be a good idea if you'd speak to Mr. Lawson and tell him to back off a bit. Tell him to give Paul a little slack. Let him have some fun."

"What has Paul told you?" she asked defensively.

"Just that his dad is acting like a marine sergeant."

"Mr. Lawson *was* a marine sergeant," she said.

"But he isn't anymore. I think Paul's uptight because his dad expects so much. Maybe you could tell Mr. Lawson not to push so hard."

She bristled and for a moment looked like she was angry and sad at the same time. "Perhaps it would be better if you tried to solve your own problems before you stuck your nose into other people's business."

"I didn't mean to . . ."

"I don't want to discuss it anymore." She returned her attention to the computer screen.

Weird, I thought. I'd never seen her act like that before. What was going on?

The phone rang and Mrs. Lawson picked it up. She was soon deep in a conversation about bus passes with somebody's parent. I tried to pick up my daydream about Rachel Parsons.

* * *

Rachel and I are dressed in leaves, walking along a white, sandy beach. The warm, tropical breeze plays lazily with her curly brown hair.

"You want me to climb a palm tree and get you a ripe, tasty coconut?" I ask Rachel.

"You'd get a ripe, tasty coconut for me?" Rachel flashes her outstanding smile. "Oh, Roob, you're just too wonderful. Nobody has ever offered to fetch me a ripe, tasty coconut before."

I tilt my head so my hair flips back. I try to look cool. "Anything for you Rachel. I'll climb a palm tree for a ripe, tasty coconut. I'll dive into the ocean for a delicious, tasty mussel."

"A mussel?" she asks.

"It's like a clam."

"Yuck."

"Okay, forget the mussel. Let's stick to coconuts. I don't want to get my hair wet anyway."

"It's getting really long," Rachel says.

"We're on a tropical island," I point out. "I can't just run into MagiCuts, can I?"

"I guess not."

"Say, Rachel, do you have any idea what *monoculture* means?" I ask.

She shakes her head, making the curls bounce. "Something to do with art and books and stuff like that?"

"Maybe," I say. "It's not important. So, do you want me to climb that tree, risk my life scaling to such a dizzy height, and pluck a ripe, juicy coconut for you?"

She looks across the deep blue tropical ocean and makes a whistling noise as she sighs through her braces. "You're just *too* wonderful, Roob. Is there anything I can do for you?"

"Well, there is one thing," I tell her.

"What is it?" she asks. "How can I repay you for a ripe, tasty coconut?"

"Well . . ." I begin.

"Yes . . ."

"Well . . ."

"Yes, what is it?" she says softly.

"Well, would you . . . would you . . . be my girlfriend?"

"Your girlfriend?"

I nod. "We're alone on this tropical island, thousands of miles from civilization, with no chance of being rescued, and I thought you could be my girlfriend."

She stares at the ocean again and smiles. The sunlight twinkles in her eyes and sparkles off her braces. "I'll think about it," she says.

* * *

Think about it?

This was *my* daydream. Why would she *think about it* in my daydream?

"I'll see you now, Robert."

I glanced up and found Mrs. Druchek, the vice-principal, glaring down at me. She definitely wasn't pleased to see me.

2

THE EIGHTH GRADE BAD DUDE

*M*rs. Druchek pointed at the open door of her office. I shuffled inside and sat on the bench against the wall.

She didn't use her chair. Instead, she half-sat, half-leaned against the side of her desk, her normal stance to dish out heck.

"Suppose you tell me what happened in Mr. Miller's class, Robert," she began.

"I was just daydreaming, ma'am," I answered. "Can I be honest?"

"I would expect it."

"To tell you the truth, Mr. Miller picks on me."

She took a deep breath. Mrs. Druchek has extremely large . . . an ample bosom. Whenever she's angry, she breathes deeply and arches her back so her chest seems larger, kind of like chickens do when they're strutting around.

"So Mr. Miller picks on you, does he?"

I nodded. "Most of the teachers do."

"I see." Mrs. Druchek breathed even deeper. "And I

suppose Mr. Raghbir was picking on you when you drew aliens in your history textbook."

"Maybe I deserved it in History."

"Was Mrs. Dawson picking on you when she asked you to stop singing in Math and you ignored her?"

"I was singing because I was in a good mood," I explained.

Truth was, I'd been thinking about Rachel Parsons. I was singing some stupid love song in my head. I didn't know I was doing it out loud, too.

"And the substitute teacher was picking on you when you threw the frog at Robert Lopez in Science?"

"The frog was dead. It was pickled. Besides, other kids were fooling around on the sub, too. It wasn't just me."

"And Mr. Simpson was picking on you when you hit him with the basketball in gym class?"

"But Mrs. Druchek, you know that was an accident. I was trying to hit James Price. James bonked me on the head with his basketball while we were practicing passes. I was just trying to get him back. Mr. Simpson got in the way."

Mrs. Druchek shook her head and made tutting sounds.

"I'll pay attention in Science from now on, ma'am," I promised.

"I'm afraid that's not good enough, Robert. This time you need to understand how inappropriate your behavior has become. You will be suspended from school for three days."

"Please don't do that, Mrs. Druchek. Mom will go gomers. You don't know how tough it is for me at home."

"I believe a few days away from Maid of the Mist ⸱⸱ School will make you appreciate us more," she

There had to be some way to get her to change her mind. "How about you place me on parole?"

"What do you mean by that?"

"Er, well, I mean, er . . ." I stuttered. "Er . . . why don't you suspend my suspension for one week. Give me five days to prove to you how good I can behave. I'll be the best student at Maid of the Mist. I'll participate in all the dumb . . ." I bit my tongue. "I mean, all the *great* school spirit stuff. I'll do my assignments on time. I'll stay out of trouble."

She stood up, walked around to the other side of the desk and sat in her chair. For several seconds she looked out the window at a girls' gym class.

I glanced out the window too. Immediately, I noticed Rachel Parsons dressed in a white T-shirt, blue gym shorts, white socks and pink sneakers. Pink. What a wonderful color for sneakers. And they looked so perfect on her.

Rachel was standing by the long jump pit with a group of other girls watching the teacher, Ms. Gomez. Rachel stood with her hands on her hips, her head bent slightly. What a super athlete.

Mrs. Druchek turned around. "All right, Robert. I'm going to give you one more chance." Then she shook her head and muttered to herself, "Though I'm not sure why."

"That's terrific," I said. "Now I'll be able to live half-peacefully with my mom."

"You have one week. If anything happens in the next five days, anything at all, then the suspension starts immediately. Do you understand what I'm saying?"

"Yes, ma'am."

"Don't disappoint me."

"No chance," I said. "I'm the new me."

* * *

Paul's mom was still wearing her angry-sad look when I left the assistant principal's office.

"Everything's okay, Mrs. L," I told her.

"I'll write up a late slip for you," she said coolly.

"Will you add five minutes to the time? I have to go to the bathroom before I go to gym."

She handed me the pink slip of paper.

"I know you're mad at me for what I said about Paul," I said as I opened the office door. "But he really has been uptight."

* * *

I went into the washroom, combed my hair and stared at myself in the mirror.

My hair was getting long. I imagined myself in a heavy-metal band and mimed air guitar in front of the mirror for half a minute. Boom-da da-da-da boom.

BOOM-DA DA-DA-DA BOOM!

I stopped being a rock star when a sixth grader came in, gave me a strange look and went into one of the cubicles.

I wondered what my father was doing. He could be writing another book in his trailer in Cape Somewhere-or-Other. Or maybe he was driving into Niagara Falls that very second. I wished he'd hurry up and get here.

I studied my reflection. I looked a lot like Dad. He had long hair, too. So long he wore it in a ponytail. We shared the same dimples when we smiled. And I had his eyes, soft gray under bushy eyebrows. Bedroom eyes, Mom called them. She said she fell in love with Dad be-
*his eyes.

*ad arrived, everything would be okay. I'd be
* him about school and Mom. And I'd be

able to tell him about my plan. I wondered how he'd react when he heard it. Would he be surprised or happy?

And I wondered if he'd changed at all. It had been a whole year. What would he be like now that he'd stopped drinking?

Dad had been a heavy drinker once. It was the reason my folks divorced. He was never mean or nasty; he just did stupid things. Like being asked to leave his teaching job for losing his students' records and sounding off at the administration. And acting stupid when company came over. Or flirting with the wives of his friends. Dumb stuff. Eventually, it got too much for Mom.

I wondered what would have happened if he hadn't entered that writing contest on the dare of one of his students? What he'd be doing if he hadn't hit it big as an author.

I looked at my watch. Still a few minutes to kill. I picked up my daydream.

* * *

Rachel and I are sitting under the coconut tree watching the gentle waves caress the beach. She's nibbling a piece of ripe, tasty coconut.

"I still don't understand why you won't be my girlfriend," I say.

"I didn't say I wouldn't," Rachel replies. "I said I'll think about it. I mean, I don't know you all that well. I was at Maid of the Mist Middle School for two whole months before we were shipwrecked, and you didn't say a word to me."

"That's 'cause I didn't know what to say. I was afraid of saying something so dumb that you'd think I was a complete dweebo."

She laughs, way up high and songlike. "Oh Roob, I'd

never do that. I'm Rachel Parsons. I'm perfect in every way. Except for my teeth, of course. But they'll be perfect when I get my braces off."

"I should have known better," I agree.

"Silly, silly Roob," she scolds.

"Would you like to go swimming?" I ask.

Her face creases into thought lines. "That would be fun. But I don't have a swimsuit."

"No problem," I grin. "You don't need one."

* * *

The sixth grader flushed away my fantasy when he flushed the toilet. He came out of the cubicle zipping up his pants, and washed his hands in the sink next to me.

After pulling a couple of paper towels from the dispenser, he smiled at me. "Hey, you're Roob Fowler. Your father is the writer, Stephen Fowler, right? My sister pointed you out to me. My teacher just finished reading one of your dad's books."

"Which one?"

"*Football Friendship*. I guess you read it, huh?"

"Not yet."

"It's good. It's about this cheerleader who falls in love with the quarterback of the high school football team. Only he doesn't love her because of the fish."

Actually, I hadn't read it because it's one of Dad's *Junior Romance Novels for Boys*. I'd hate to be seen walking around with a *romance* story. I don't believe in that starry-eyed junk.

The sixth grader reached into his shirt pocket, pulled out a pack of Hubba Bubba Fruit Punch bubble gum and offered me a piece.

"Thanks," I said as I peeled the wrapper. "You want to know something? When I was a little kid I used to swallow gum. Once I swallowed so much gum the doctor had to cut my stomach open to get it out. They cut me from my crotch to my throat."

"You're kidding?" the kid gasped.

"I had a piece of gum stuck in my small intestine the size of a softball."

"You're kidding!"

"Yeah."

"Yeah?"

"Yeah, I'm kidding."

"Oh." He seemed disappointed.

"It's a good story though, isn't it? I'm going to be a writer when I leave school. Just like my dad."

"It must be great to have a father who's famous."

"It is. He's real cool."

"Can I come over to your place and visit him?" the sixth grader wondered.

"He doesn't live with us."

"My parents are divorced, too," the kid told me. "My father lives in Chicago. Where does yours live?"

"Wherever he wants. He has a 4x4 and a trailer. He drives around and parks in a different campground every month or so. He's been all over the States and Canada, even to Alaska. That's where he gets his ideas for new stories."

"Narly." The sixth grader reached into his pocket and pulled out a half-chewed pen. "Would you sign my arm?"

"Your arm?"

"The kids in my class will be impressed if you do," he said.

Why not? I thought. I scrawled my signature across his forearm.

"I can't read it," he complained. "You make your F's funny. It looks like Boob Bowler."

I wasn't going to take that. "You want me to sign your face with my fist, Tadpole Breath?"

The kid backed up. "Sorry, I didn't mean to make you mad."

"Apology accepted."

"I hear you're the eighth grade bad dude," the sixth grader continued. "I hear you're the guy who trashed the Coke machine in the cafeteria last Christmas."

I shrugged. "It was an accident. The can was stuck and I was shaking the machine to get it out. I shook too hard and it fell over."

"I heard you kicked it over."

I shook my head. "That's not true. How do rumors like that start? It was an accident. They should nail soda machines to the floor."

"Was it an accident when you pushed the piano off the stage too?"

"Of course it was. I was moving props for the Christmas Concert and didn't know how close the edge of the stage was."

Actually, I was goofing around and not paying attention, but it was still an accident . . . a spectacular and noisy accident.

He held out his hand. "My name's Chad."

I shook it. It was still wet.

"I'll see you around," he said.

After he left the washroom, I wiped my moist hand on my jeans and checked my watch again. There were only ten minutes left of gym. Good, Mr. Simpson wouldn't make me get changed now. I looked at myself in the mirror for the last time.

"You can do it, Robert, my man," I said. "You can be the eighth grade *good dude* for five days. It's only one week."

3

THE TRACK TEAM?

*B*y the time I got a drink from the fountain, grabbed my gym strip from my locker and walked slowly down the hall to the gym, Mr. Simpson was sending the class to the showers. I'd timed it perfectly.

"Sorry, I'm late, Mr. Simpson," I said as I swallowed the gum and handed my late slip to him.

He didn't bother to look at it. "I'd like to see you in my office for a minute, Robert. I want to talk to you about something."

Did he know I was dawdling in the washroom? If he told Mrs. Druchek, I'd be finished before I started.

I followed him through the gym office door and sat down in a chair while he squeezed his large gut behind his desk.

Mr. Simpson rested his hands on his ample abdomen and studied me for several seconds. "Why don't you like gym class, Robert?" he asked finally.

Was this some kind of trick question? "It's not you, Mr. Simpson," I answered. "You're the best gym teacher I've ever had. You're the best gym teacher in the school, maybe in the whole city."

He held up his hand to stop me. "I don't need the bull. Just answer the question."

"Okay, sir. It's simple really. I'm not crazy about gym because I think it's sort of stupid to get dressed in baggy shorts and run around until I'm out of breath and all sweaty."

I thought about Rachel Parsons running and sweaty and out of breath. That wouldn't be stupid.

"Your poor attitude toward physical education is a crime. A pure waste," Mr. Simpson said bluntly. "It's a waste of your natural talent."

"I'll try harder next class," I said.

Mr. Simpson went on. "You're slender. You're coordinated. I've watched you in class. Have you ever played on a sports team?"

"I tried playing hockey when I was in second grade," I told him. "I got kicked out because I kept tripping and hitting the players with my stick."

"I can see the other team getting upset by that style of play."

"I did it to my team, too. I'm just not a team guy."

"Maybe it's time to change that." Mr. Simpson leaned back in the chair. "I'm sure I'm close to coaching the best junior four-hundred-meter relay team in Niagara Falls. Maybe in the whole of New York. I think we're state contenders this year. I can feel it. This is going to be our year."

"I'm real happy about that." I tried hard to sound enthusiastic.

"The Price twins, James and John, have shown a lot of improvement over the past month," Mr. Simpson told me. "And I'm almost positive Robert Lopez will be Olympic material someday."

"They're great guys." I nearly choked on those words.

"And Paul Lawson has impressed me too," Mr. Simpson

continued. "Another week of training and he'll be right with us."

"He's my best friend."

"But I need another man." Mr. Simpson sounded as if someone had just run over and squashed his dog with an eighteen-wheeler. "Several of your classmates have tried for the spot, but so far nobody has the right stuff. I need a natural runner. I need *you*. I want you to consider being on my relay team. I want you to consider bringing glory to Maid of the Mist Middle School and the city of Niagara Falls."

"Me? On the relay team?"

"Don't say *no* right away, Robert. Think seriously about it over the weekend and give me your answer on Monday."

"I'm not interes . . ." I stopped.

Yes!

This was my chance to show Mrs. Druchek I'd reformed.

Mr. Simpson placed his hands palm down on his desk. "I'll see you on Monday morning."

"I don't have to think about it, sir," I said as I stood up. "I'll do it. I'd be proud to be on the relay team."

It took him a moment to understand what I'd said. "You would?"

"Practice today, Coach? Right after school?"

"Not today," he answered. "Friday nights I play basketball for the Legion."

"Too bad." I hoped I sounded sincere.

"But there's a voluntary practice tomorrow at three," he explained. "Can you make that?"

"Tomorrow? Saturday? You practice on a weekend?"

"Like I said, I have great hopes for this team. We want to be ready."

"On Saturday?"

"It's voluntary."

"Saturday?"

"Do you have plans?"

I shook my head.

"The other boys would appreciate it." He paused. "*I'll* appreciate it."

I thought about Mrs. Druchek's deal. "I'll be here," I announced.

"That's outstanding, Robert." His face formed a wide smile.

"No sweat, Coach. Could I ask you to do me a favor though? Before you go home, could you tell Mrs. Druchek I want to be on the team? Could you tell her I want to be a runner for Maid of the Mist real bad?"

"If you wish. I'm sure she'll be happy to hear it."

* * *

"I don't understand why you're not happy I didn't get booted out," I said to Paul on the walk home from school. "Now my mom won't dump on me."

"I'm happy about that," he said, shuffling his knapsack from one shoulder to the other. "It's you being on the track team that worries me."

"Why? It's a great way to earn suck-up points."

"Now there are too many people," he reasoned. "James and John Price, Bob Lopez, you and me. That's five. Only four guys can run. Mr. Simpson will have to cut somebody. That could be me."

"Maybe I won't make it."

Paul shook his head. "Mr. Simpson wouldn't have asked you if he didn't think you were better than one of us."

"The way Simpson explained it, he was looking for another body. He didn't say he was going to drop anybody. In fact, he said nice things about you. Maybe he wants me to be a sub."

"Or maybe I'll get to be the sub."

"So what's wrong with that?" I asked.

"It won't be good enough for my dad." He sighed. "Being a sub is like being a water boy to him. He's already invited my grandparents from Rochester to watch the city meet in two weeks. He'd die of embarrassment if I was just a sub."

"That doesn't make sense."

"Tell me about it." Paul shuffled his knapsack again.

"How come you're carrying the contents of your locker home?" I asked.

He looked at me as if he couldn't believe what I'd just said. "Get serious. We have four pages of math, a sheet of English questions, the science project and a history test to study for. How come you're not carrying the same truckload of books?"

I smiled. "I'll copy your math and English first thing Monday morning. The science project isn't due until Thursday and I'm flunking history, so there's no use studying for the test."

"I wish I could think like that, Roob. My life would be so much easier."

"I just say to myself, 'Will I die if I don't do this?' If the answer is *no*, then it's not really that important."

"My answer would always have to be *yes*," he said. "You know my dad would kill me if I didn't get top marks. I have to show him all my assignments every single day now. If he doesn't think they're neat enough, I have to rewrite them."

"How long has he been doing that?"

"A couple of weeks. Ever since I got a B+ on the science test. He's getting worse, Roob. I have to go to bed at 9:30. He's even started to tell me what to eat."

"You're kidding."

"I feel like I'm in prison. Last night he made up his own math test to give me."

"Wow."

"He called Mrs. Dawson when I *only* got 96 percent on the last assignment."

"I got 26 percent."

"He knows."

"He knows? How does your dad know what my math mark was?"

"He asked Dawson."

"Why?"

"Because he'd been bugging me to find new friends. He thinks you're a bad influence. I told him you and I are friends for life. Right?"

"Right," I agreed. "Why don't you do what I suggested a while ago? Why don't you shout and scream. That always gets my mom's attention."

"I've tried. Dad shouts and screams back. You know how scary he is when he's angry."

"He's scary when he's happy. It's too bad your father can't be more like mine. My dad doesn't hassle me."

"That's 'cause you only see him once a year."

"I'm going to see if I can change that," I said. "I'm going to see if I can live with Dad."

"In his trailer?" Paul puzzled. "How are you going to do that?"

"When my folks split up, I remember them saying when I got old enough I could choose who to live with. Well, I figure I'm old enough now."

"Maybe. But how can you go to school if you're driving around the country in a trailer?"

"I can take my courses by mail," I told him. "The state has a correspondence school for kids who study at home."

"No kidding?"

"I'll tool around North America with Dad. Whenever

he writes, I'll do school work. Neat, huh? I can spend the winter where it's warm."

"You told your mom yet?"

"No, but I don't think she'll care. You know how we've been arguing lately."

"I'm not sure. Won't she think you don't want to live with her anymore? Won't that hurt her feelings?"

"I don't know. Look, don't say nothing to your folks, okay? Not until I talk to Dad. I don't want Mom to know about it."

We strolled up Paul's driveway. "I'll miss you if you move away, Roob. We've been friends since the first day I moved into the neighborhood. I still remember you sitting on your BMX bike staring at the movers."

"I was trying to see what toys you had, to see if you were worth playing with."

He smiled slightly. "We were one of the first black families in the neighborhood and I was so nervous about it. I thought nobody would want to play with me. I was so glad when you came up and said hello."

"That's because the movers unloaded your Ping-Pong table. I wanted to play Ping-Pong."

He smiled a little more. "You're the only person who can make me laugh."

"Well, I haven't been doing much of that lately, have I?" I pointed out. "What do you say we go to the mall tonight? Go to a movie, check out the old baseball cards and comics in the store. See who shows up?"

He shook his head. "I can't. I have to do my homework tonight."

"You're the only person on the whole planet who does homework on Friday night," I said. "Do it Sunday night like everybody else."

"I've got too much," Paul explained. "I've got my guitar

lesson tomorrow morning and track practice in the afternoon. That doesn't leave a lot of time."

"How about we go for a walk around Goat Island then. Your dad would let you take an hour off to do that, wouldn't he?"

"I don't know," Paul hedged. "I can ask him."

Paul climbed his front steps, and I was about to turn and walk back down the driveway. "Your father is too strict," I said. "Maybe I'll ask my dad if you can live in his trailer too."

Paul opened the screen door and lowered his voice as if he was telling me a secret. "You know, I wonder what my father would do if he didn't have me to order around?"

"You thinking of running away?"

"No," he said softly. "Something else."

"What?"

"Something to scare him. Do you think if I scared him, he'd leave me alone?"

"Scare him? What are you talking about."

"Maybe someday he'll push me to it."

"Come on, man," I said. "Do you know how weird you sound?"

He nodded. "Yeah, it's all weird when you think about it, isn't it?"

There was something in the way he said that sentence, flat and dull, robot-like, that made a tingling shiver crawl up my spine.

"See you, later, good buddy," he said as he opened the door and went into his house.

4

MOM

Supper was almost ready when Mom got home from work. She changed into her sweats and sat at the kitchen table.

"Dinner is served," I announced, making a waiter-type flourish and placing a steaming plate in front of her. "Tuna Helper. Only I used the left-over chicken from last night instead of tuna." I put another plate on my place mat and pulled up a chair.

I'd been helping with dinner so Mom wouldn't grump so much. I was sick of hearing, "I work eight hours a day and then I face a dirty house, two loads of laundry and a hungry family to feed."

A hungry family is an exaggeration. There's only me and my sixteen-year-old sister, Helen, who's seldom home to eat supper anyway. Helen is into cheerleading and a certain basketball player named Woody. She puts on the feed bag at Woody's house most of the time.

Mom unfolded a paper napkin and placed it on her lap. "The kitchen looks tidy."

I also made sure I cleaned up my breakfast dishes. Mom is a cleanliness nut. Our house has to be like a hospital or else she goes on a cleaning rampage. You can't even talk to her in her "cleaning mode." I made a mental note to do my bedroom. It had been a couple of weeks since she inspected it last.

"How was work?" I asked.

"I received a call from your school at K Mart this afternoon."

I banged my fork on the table. "Nuts, I didn't think Mrs. Druchek would do that."

Mom looked puzzled. "Mrs. Druchek didn't call. Why would Mrs. Druchek want to talk to me?"

"Er . . . well, I . . . er . . . I didn't think she'd phone you just to say I'd joined the track team."

Mom's face brightened. "Pardon me?"

"I joined the four-hundred-meter relay team. The one Paul is on."

"That's wonderful," she beamed. "When did you decide to do that?"

"When Mr. Simpson asked me this afternoon. He says I'm a natural runner. I've got my first practice tomorrow. On Saturday." No need to explain the probation stuff, I thought.

"Well," Mom said. "This almost makes up for the phone call from Mrs. Dawson."

"Mrs. Dawson? I can't believe it. My math teacher bugged you while you were doing your important work."

"Don't be sarcastic," Mom warned. "It may not be *important* work, but it pays okay and it feeds this family."

I smiled. "It's *very* important to work in the women's underwear section at K Mart. If it wasn't for you, there'd be thousands of women walking around Niagara Falls in old, ratty underwear."

Even though she didn't want to, Mom smiled too. "A horrible thought." Then she tried to look serious. "I'm still upset about the call."

"What did Old Lady Dawson want? I haven't been doing anything in Math."

"Don't call her *Old Lady* Dawson."

"It's true."

"It's not nice."

"Okay, why would *Elderly* Mrs. Dawson call you?"

"You're being rude, Robert," Mom said. "You never used to be this way. You've been so different lately."

"Don't start, Mom. Let's not get upset at each other for once."

"I'm *not* starting. I just want you to know how I feel. I feel my son is growing up to be a stranger. I can't believe you're the same little bundle I used to breast-feed."

"Don't talk about that," I complained. "We're eating. It's mondo gross."

"Well, you are different, Rob."

I grinned. "No, I'm not. I'm still the same person who used to give the cat a bath in the toilet."

Mom couldn't help but chuckle at the memory. When she laughs she looks really young, and I can picture what she must have been like when she was a teenager. It's too bad she doesn't laugh more often. "Bootsie was such a great cat. Why she didn't scratch you, I'll never know."

"That's because I used to bonk her on the head with a Tonka truck before I picked her up."

"You what?" Mom sounded shocked.

"I used to hit Bootsie on the head with my toys. It made her dopey. That's why she didn't scratch me."

"I . . . what? You used to hit poor Bootsie?"

I shook my head. "No, I'm just joking. I'd never do anything like that. I was just making up a story. You know, practicing to be a writer, like Dad."

Mom released a long breath. "I worry about you, Robert."

I answered with Dad's favorite saying, "Don't worry about me. I'm just crazy."

"I hate that."

"Sorry. I have Dad's sense of humor. Tell me why Old La . . . why Mrs. Dawson called you."

She placed her fork on her plate and folded her hands on the edge of the table. "Mrs. Dawson told me you've been doing very little in Math. She says unless your work improves you might fail her class."

"Math is so boring, Mom. We're studying stupid geometry."

"It isn't *stupid*. If it wasn't important, they wouldn't teach it."

"Dad says most of the stuff we do at school is stupid."

"I wish your father wouldn't say things like that. It's given you a bad attitude."

"Dad says there's nothing wrong with my attitude. He says the rest of the world sucks."

"Another of his drunken comments," she grumbled.

"It was not," I defended. "He said it on the phone a couple of months ago. Dad doesn't drink anymore."

She bit her bottom lip, then sighed. "Robert, your father is an alcoholic. It's the reason he's not part of our family anymore."

"He *was* an alcoholic. He isn't anymore. He quit drinking last year."

"Oh he's still drinking all right. I can tell by his voice."

I remembered the phone calls Mom was talking about. Dad *had* sounded different. But it wasn't because he was drunk. "He had a cold then. And the other time he was just tired."

"Tired after a bottle of Scotch."

I was getting angry. I forced it down and tried to change the subject. "Do you think he'll arrive soon? He said he was going to be here by now."

"How should I know? If your father cared about his children he'd be more definite about his plans, wouldn't he?"

I lost it. "That's not fair!" I shouted. "Dad cares about Helen and me. And he doesn't drink anymore."

"I don't know what I ever saw in that man," she grumbled.

"Well, you must have liked him for a few minutes," I said sarcastically, "or else I wouldn't be here."

She unfolded her hands and thumped them on either side of her plate. "I like babies a lot more than big kids."

The phone rang and Mom left the table to get it. I hoped it was Dad, but I heard her say, "Hello, Dennis . . ."

I wasn't interested in hearing half a conversation with Dennis the construction worker, her current boyfriend, so I thought about Rachel Parsons.

I wondered what Rachel was doing right at that moment. She was probably in her bedroom, sprawled on her bed. Maybe she was reading one of my father's novels. If only I could be there with her. I could tell her my dad had written the book. Would she ever be impressed.

Mom returned to the table.

"How's Dennis?" I asked.

"Fine." She picked up her fork again, but didn't eat anything. "I love you, Robert. And you know I'll always be there to help you. But I really wish you would do better in school. You're so intelligent, but you never get anything higher than a C. You need to do well in middle school so you can get into the academic program in high school."

"You've told me this at least six times."

"Then why don't you listen?"

"School is boring. I can learn everything by reading

the *Note to Teachers* page at the beginning of each textbook."

She sighed. "It's not only your marks; it's your behavior too. You always seem to be getting into trouble."

"The teachers pick on me. Every time I make one measly little mistake, they make a big deal out of it."

"Setting fire to one of the outside lunch tables is not a *measly little* mistake," Mom said.

"That was last October. And you know I didn't do it on purpose. I was just burning my initials into the wood with a magnifying glass. I didn't know the paint would flare up like that."

"And I suppose you consider burning your initials into school property appropriate behavior?"

"I bought the school a new table out of my gift money. It was last fall. How come you're bringing it up now?"

She reared back as if she was ready to explode, ready to throw the A-bomb of parental lectures into my face.

But her shoulders suddenly slumped. "What's the use? What can I tell you that I haven't already said a hundred times before?" Her voice dropped almost to a whisper. "I don't know what to do with you anymore. Maybe I should sign you up with Uncles for Friends."

"What?"

"Uncles for Friends," she explained. "It pairs male volunteers to boys without fathers. Maybe if you had a man to talk to, it would help."

"Where would you get such a stupid idea?" I almost shouted. "I have a father. If I want to talk to somebody, it'll be to him."

"How many weeks has it been since he called you last?"

"Dad's busy!" I yelled. "Dad's busy doing . . ."

But for some reason I couldn't make the words. Something inside reached up and grabbed my throat. A trickle of tears slid over my cheeks.

Mom reached across the table and squeezed my hand. "I'm sorry, Robert."

"I'm going to my room," I said. "I'm not hungry anymore."

* * *

I sat on the end of my bed and looked at the stuff on my shelves.

"Things are a mess," I said to the teddy bear I'd had since day one.

The ratty stuffed animal just stared back at me.

"I'm going to go live with Dad. Everything has got crazy this year, Ted. Maybe Mom is right. Maybe I *am* different. I sure feel like I don't fit around here anymore."

I smiled at the old Teenage Mutant Ninja Turtle action figures on the same shelf. "I'm too big to play with you guys. I wonder why I keep you around."

I stood up and rubbed my hand across my Sega Genesis. "Maybe I'll give you to Paul as a good-bye gift. Paul could use a little fun in his life. It's too bad about his dad. We all have our problems."

I saluted the old Rolling Stones poster Dad had given me. They weren't bad for a bunch of guys as old as dinosaurs. "You know, Mick, when I come back to visit, I'm going to be a lot happier."

Then to my surprise, I sucked in a deep breath and another wash of tears flowed across my cheeks. "I'm sure going to miss Mom. She tried so hard to fill in for Dad. She's tried to be patient about school. I'm going to hate leaving her."

I wiped at the tears. This was no good. If I started

thinking about Mom, I might change my mind about living with Dad.

The phone rang again. This time it was Paul. Mom called me and I got the extension in Helen's bedroom.

"You okay?" Paul asked after I said hello. "You sound stuffy."

"I've been arguing with my mom," I told him.

"Oh." He went silent for a few seconds. "Anyway, my father has decided to unlock my chains for an hour. He says I'm allowed to go to Goat Island with you as long as I have my homework finished. He says I can finish my science project Sunday."

"Great. When will you be done?"

"Call on me in an hour," he answered. "You know, Roob, if Dad had said *no*, I would have sneaked out."

That surprised me. "Sneaked out? You'd do that?"

"There's a lot of stuff I'm thinking of doing," he said.

Just like when we were at his front door, electricity sizzled along my backbone.

5

JERK

An hour later, I hiked to Paul's house, three blocks away. His father opened the door wearing his usual disapproving look.

"Come in," he ordered.

Paul's dad is tall with a great build for a guy pushing forty. When I was younger, I was scared of him. Mr. Lawson spent a few years in the marines and made it to the rank of sergeant. He obviously spent a lot of time staring new recruits down because the mean-and-ugly look is chiseled into his face.

He didn't invite me into the living room. We stood in the hallway. He frowned and I tried to smile. "Paul will be another few minutes," he told me. "One page of his math was untidy so I'm making him do it over." Then he sucked in a deep breath, making his nostrils flare. "Mrs. Lawson tells me that you believe I'm being too strict with Paul."

"She said that?"

He nodded slowly, while he glared at me from under his arched eyebrows.

"I guess I do think that," I explained. "I don't want to

make you mad or anything, Mr. L. It's just that Paul is more than a little stressed out."

"I believe Mrs. Lawson told you it was none of your business."

"Sorry. I only said it because Paul is my friend. I care about him."

"So do I, I'm his father." He paused, rubbed his chin a couple of times. "I'm not sure why I'm having this conversation with you. I think you're too young to understand. But I am helping Paul."

"Maybe, Mr. L, but he's sure unhappy," I said.

Mr. Lawson's nostrils flared again. "That may be. For now. He may feel I'm being too strict with him, but he'll thank me for it one day."

I didn't understand that at all.

"Do you know what I do for a living, Robert?"

"Sure, you're a manager for the city."

"I order supplies. I make sure the city has enough lawn mowers to cut the grass in the parks. I make sure there are enough trash cans on street corners. I make sure there are enough manhole covers. Does that sound like a good job to you?"

I shrugged. "Beats working in the women's underwear section in K Mart, I guess."

"It's a boring job," he said flatly. "I hate every minute of it. But I have no other skills. I can't quit because I'd never be able to find another job at the same salary. I don't want Paul to grow up and find himself in the same position. Do you understand?"

"Not really."

"I want Paul to go to college, graduate and get a job that he likes and that pays well. I can't afford the best colleges in this country. Paul will need a scholarship. The only way he can get one is if he maintains top marks through high school. Now do you understand?"

"Sort of."

"I'm pushing Paul because if I don't he'll lose the opportunity to become more than I am. When he becomes a lawyer or a doctor or an engineer or whatever other profession he chooses, he'll thank me for being so strict with him today."

"I get it, Mr. L. But Paul's a top student anyway. He already knows how to get A's. Maybe if you praised him instead of scaring him, you'd . . ."

"I beg your pardon," he interrupted. "I do not *scare* my son."

I felt really uncomfortable. But Paul was my best friend. Best friends look out for each other. "Paul's frightened of what you'll say and do if he doesn't make the track team."

"Perhaps it wasn't a good idea to discuss this with you. You're definitely too young to understand."

"I'm listening to you, sir."

"Paul will get the chances that passed me by. In high school, I was a top sprinter. I could have raced with the best in the world if somebody had given me a boot in the pants. But nobody pushed me. My coach was white, and he made sure he gave most of his time to the white boys. My step-father couldn't care less. I care about Paul and want to make sure his chances don't slip away."

Paul came down the stairs already dressed in his Reeboks and jacket. He handed a sheet of math to his father.

"Much better," Mr. Lawson said after checking it. "You may go out now."

* * *

I've never lived anywhere other than Niagara Falls. Like me, my folks are Canadian. They met when they were both summer students working at Ripley's Museum. I was born in Niagara Falls, Canada, and lived there until I was in first grade. Then my dad got famous and decided he'd like to live Stateside for a change.

I'm only a five-minute bus ride from the Falls themselves. The Niagara River splits into two waterfalls, the Horseshoe, half in Canada and half in the U.S., and the American, all in the States. Paul and I like to walk around Goat Island, the piece of land separating the two falls.

I never get tired of seeing them. Or hearing them. Their sound is so hypnotizing, a constant thundering roar so overwhelming I can feel it in my teeth.

We got off the bus and crossed the pedestrian bridge connecting Goat Island to the mainland. There wasn't anybody else around. May 3 was still early in the season. Come the May long weekend, the place would be swarming with tourists.

At first, I liked it that we were the only ones there. Paul stopped and leaned over the railing. I leaned beside him. The water rushed a car's-length beneath us. We watched it rage and foam over the rocks as it surged toward the edge of the American Falls two hundred meters away.

"So what's the big secret?" Paul asked. "Tell me what you and Dad were talking about."

"Not much." I wasn't sure how Paul would react if he found out I'd been talking to his folks about how strict they were.

"It was me, wasn't it? Was he telling you I need to study more?"

"Not really."

"I know," Paul guessed. "He was telling you I was going to get the chances he missed, right?"

"Yeah. Kind of."

"Wish I had a buck for every time I hear that speech."

I still didn't want to confess I'd been poking my nose into his family. I thought I was doing right, but he might think I was out of line. So we continued to watch the current swirl downstream.

"It's really moving fast tonight," Paul noted.

"There's been a lot of rain in Ohio," I told him. "And there was a lot of snow up in Canada last winter. Lake Erie is two inches higher than normal."

He straightened up. "How come you know that and you don't have any idea what monoculture means?"

I shrugged. "I find the news interesting. It's like reading a book. You never know what's going to happen next. What is monoculture anyway?"

"It means the farmer has only one crop growing in the whole field."

"That doesn't have much to do with kissing, does it?"

"Watch this," he said. And to my shock, he hoisted his leg over the railing and straddled it like he was riding a horse.

"What are you doing?" I blurted. "Don't be crazy."

"Crazy?" He arched his eyebrows and laughed as if I'd just told him a joke. "Crazy? This isn't crazy. This is." And with that, keeping his hands tight on the rail, he lifted his other leg over. He stood on the few centimeters of concrete directly over the raging river.

My mouth dried up, leaving a metallic taste on my tongue. I couldn't believe what he was doing. "Paul? Don't be nuts. You could fall. There's no way you can swim in there. You'd go over the Falls."

He laughed again. "I know."

"You'd be killed on the rocks." My voice came out shaky. "This isn't funny, Paul."

He straightened his arms and leaned out over the water. "What would you tell my father, Roob? What would you say to him?"

"Get back on the bridge, man." I stepped forward and made a motion to grab him.

"Don't!" he warned. "Don't touch me."

I stopped. "Don't scare me like this, Paul." I looked around, hoping to see somebody who could help me. But there was no one. I wasn't happy we were alone anymore.

"I wonder what my father would say when you told him, Roob."

"Please, Paul. I'm not impressed. Stop this."

He stood there, leaning back, wearing a weird half-smile on his face. The water danced and swirled beneath him.

"Please, man," I begged.

His half-smile turned into a toothy grin. "Okay, good buddy." He hoisted himself back over the railing.

I released a breath from the bottom of my feet and slapped his shoulder. "You stupid jerk. What was all that about?"

He continued to grin. "You sure looked scared."

I slapped his shoulder a second time. "Of course I was. That's the dumbest thing you've ever done. What got into you?"

The grin vanished, replaced by a tight-eyed stare. "I don't know. Sometimes I get to thinking. I wonder what my father would do if I . . . I don't know, did something he'd never, ever expect me to do."

"I think you should talk to Mr. Welles."

"The school counselor? You think I need help?"

"Yeah. Hanging off a bridge over the Niagara River is not normal."

"Don't worry about me."

"I'm just crazy," I added in my head.

"Come on," he said. "Let's walk."

"That was weird, man," I said. "Majorly weird."

We crossed the bridge and turned right, taking the pathway to the edge of the American Falls.

"My little cousin, Brad, read one of your father's *Boy Scout Buddies* books," Paul said. "That's the very first book he's ever read by himself. He really liked it. He wants to read all the others."

I was looking at my hands. They were still shaking. "I'll tell Dad when he comes. He likes to hear stuff like that."

I felt stupid talking about Dad's books. So we walked in silence for a while. After what had just happened, I didn't know what to say to him.

"Do you like Amber Littlewood?" Paul asked.

"She's okay. Why?"

"I think she likes me," he said. "I was reading an Archie comic at lunch. From out of nowhere, Amber came over to me, pointed at Chuck and told me she thinks Chuck is really cute."

"So what?"

"So she was flirting with me. That was her way of telling me *I* was cute. Chuck is black, right?"

"This is just too bizarre, Paul. I feel strange talking about a girl after what you did at the bridge."

He waved off my concern. "Seems like a good thing to talk about to me. Amber's sort of pretty, huh?"

"I just . . ."

"Come on, Roob. We're out for a walk. Talk to me. Amber's pretty, right?"

I sighed. "Yeah, Amber's cute. But only a tenth as cute as Rachel Parsons."

"If you think Rachel is so wonderful, why don't you talk to her?"

It still didn't feel right making small talk. "I'm shy."

He chuckled. "You're lots of things. Shy isn't one of them."

"I can't just walk up to her," I said. "That would be too obvious. I'm trying to think of the right thing to say."

"How about, 'Can I have fries with that?'"

"Huh?"

"I saw her working at the Burger Baron in the mall last Saturday," Paul said. "Why don't you go there for lunch tomorrow? That would be a good excuse to talk to her."

I thought about it. "Yeah, it would, wouldn't it?"

The path wound up from the riverbank and led through trees. The maples, beeches and oaks were in full bud, but lots of evening sunshine still reached us. Then the trail eased back to the river.

Part of the bank had eroded, exposing the roots of a couple of red maples. One of them tilted at an angle over the river like a diving board. In my imagination, I pictured Paul playing chicken by running out on the trunk.

To my relief, he didn't. In fact, he seemed really calm, as if he didn't understand he'd just risked his life.

The current appeared to pick up speed as it moved closer to the drop. The rumble of the Falls washed through me. I could almost believe the water was anxious to smash itself into spray on the rocks below.

We reached the edge, and for the hundredth time I watched the torrent of water spilling violently into the gorge below. I got this chilling image of my friend waving to me as he was swept into the middle of the bubbling rush.

The spray wet our hair and my bangs fell in wet rattails in front of my eyes. I began to shiver, but I wasn't sure it was from the cold.

A busload of elderly tourists with southern accents arrived and pushed in front of us. We began walking back to the bridge.

"Guess I'll go home and tell Dad you're on the track team now," Paul said. "I wonder what he'll say."

"I've been thinking about this track team thing," I told him. "I may have an idea that'll help both of us."

"Yeah?"

"What if, tomorrow at the practice, I fake a sprained ankle. I could pull a wipe while running. That way I still get points for being on the team and it makes sure you're not the sub."

He threw his arm around my shoulder. "Dishonest. Nasty. But I like it. A great plan. My father will be happy. What favor can I do in return?"

"You can promise no more craziness like at the bridge."

He began patting my shoulder. "If my father had seen me he would have done a dump in his pants, wouldn't he?"

I was really anxious as we walked back across the bridge. I was half-expecting Paul to repeat his stunt. When he saw the look on my face, he smiled. "Don't worry about me," he repeated.

6

A BRIBE AND A BURGER

I had a hard time falling asleep. Usually I drift off thinking about Rachel Parsons and all the great things we could do if she and I had a week in Disney World. But I just couldn't picture me and Rachel and Donald Duck that night.

Paul kept me awake. I couldn't shake the image of my friend dangling off the bridge. I ran the worst-case scenario through my mind over and over. Him slipping off, bobbing and thrashing in the river as the current swept toward the edge.

It was just crazy. I had to talk to somebody about him. If I told Mom, she'd call his folks. That would freak them out and make his life more miserable. First thing Monday, I'd make an appointment to see Mr. Welles, tell the counselor what happened. He'd know what to do. Paul would be furious, of course. But so what?

* * *

I spent Saturday morning numbed out on TV cartoons. I was too tired to do anything else.

"Do you want me to make you a sandwich?" Mom asked at lunchtime.

"No," I answered. "I'm going to walk down to the mall. I'll grab something down there."

As I was walking down my driveway, I was surprised when Paul's dad pulled up to the curb.

He leaned over and opened the passenger door. "Hello, Robert," he called. "I'm glad I caught you. Can I offer you a ride?"

"I'm going to the mall."

"Hop in."

I climbed in and closed the door. "Thanks, Mr. L."

"My pleasure. I was hoping to find you in," he said as he put the car in gear. "I'll come right to the point. Paul told me you're on the track team now. I want you off."

"Off the team? Why?"

He reached into the inside pocket of his sports jacket, pulled out an envelope and handed it to me. "This is for you."

There was nothing written on the outside, so I flipped open the flap. Inside were two $100 bills.

I stared at the money. "This is for me?"

Mr. Lawson turned down Grand Boulevard and headed toward the mall. "It's your money if you tell the coach you're no longer interested in being a member of the Maid of the Mist four-hundred-meter relay team."

"I don't understand, Mr. L. You'll give me two hundred bucks if I drop out of track?"

"Don't play dim, Robert. You know exactly what's going on here. I'm buying you out. With you on the team, someone else has to be dropped. I don't want that someone to be Paul."

"Maybe that won't happen. I might not make the team. And if I do, Mr. Simpson will still need a sub. Maybe nobody will be dropped."

"Being a substitute is not good enough for my son. It's important to me that Paul makes the team."

"Why don't you offer the money to Robert Lopez or one of the Price twins. Why me? Paul and I are good friends."

"The reason I'm offering the money to you is because Paul told me you joined to impress Mrs. Druchek. You couldn't care less about the track team."

I couldn't argue with that.

"But you do care about money."

I couldn't argue with that either.

"Take the money, Robert."

I was stunned. Nothing like this had ever happened to me before. What Mr. Lawson was doing wasn't right. It wasn't fair to Mr. Simpson. It wasn't fair to the other guys on the team. And it definitely wasn't fair to Paul.

Then I realized that what I was planning to do that afternoon, fake a sprained ankle, was a pretty crummy thing to do too. It was just as unfair.

"Take the money," Mr. Lawson said.

I tossed the envelope on the dash board. "I don't want it. I couldn't spend it because it would make me feel as slimy as you." I waited and then added a sarcastic, "Sir."

I had to fight the wave of anxiety flying around in my guts. I'd never spoken to Paul's dad that way. I had no idea how he was going to react. Like Paul said, Mr. Lawson was pretty scary when he was mad.

"You're making a grave mistake," Mr. Lawson growled.

"You don't have to worry about me being on the team. I'll drop out, but for my own reasons."

Paul's father pulled into the mall parking lot. "A wise choice. And I'm surprised, Robert. You actually seem to have some kind of sense of right and wrong."

"Which is more than I can say for you. I guess Paul gets his chances whatever they cost, huh?" It took an awful lot of courage to say that. I half-expected Mr.

Lawson to reach over, slap me on the head and tell me to smarten up.

Instead, he stopped the car and looked at me with his marine sergeant expression.

For a moment, I was going to snitch on Paul. I was going to tell Mr. Lawson about what happened on the bridge last night. But I couldn't. Mr. Lawson would probably have a fit. There was no telling what he'd do to Paul.

"You know, Mr. Lawson, you may think I'm just a dumb kid, but I know one thing you don't. All this pressure you're putting on Paul isn't good. He's got a problem. I'd sit down and have a good talk with him if I were you. There's definitely some things you and Paul should discuss."

He didn't respond. He just continued to stare at me with his I'm-going-to-break-your-butt expression.

"Say hello to Paul for me," I said as I got out of the car.

* * *

The Food Fair was full of people. Families, kids and old folks were lined up in front of the food counters.

I was upset about the conversation with Paul's father. But I had something important to do, perhaps the most important thing I'd ever do in my entire life. I was going to talk to Rachel Parsons for the first time. I did my best to shove the Lawson family to the back of my mind.

I looked around, found an empty table and sat down. At first I couldn't see who was serving at the Burger Baron because of the crowd. Then the people parted and there she was, just like Paul had said, smiling at the customers, showing her soon-to-be-perfect teeth.

Rachel Parsons wore a purple vest and the little purple paper crown all Burger Baron employees wear. Even in something so dopey, she looked terrific.

Just like the first time I saw her, I thought. It was in the school lunchroom. I walked in and there she was, the new kid, sitting with her new classmates, chewing on a ham and cheese sandwich. She had a dab of mustard on the end of her nose. Not even angels could be so good-looking.

The customers shuffled in front of Rachel again, hiding her. Unable to see the real thing, I returned to the island and picked up my fantasy . . .

* * *

"What do you mean I don't need a swimsuit?" Rachel asks. "How can I go swimming without one?"

I'm still grinning. "Nobody is going to see you. Remember, you're thousands of miles away from the nearest person."

"I don't understand," she says.

"Well," I explain, "you could, er . . . you could, er . . ."

"I could what?" she interrupts.

"You could, well . . . you could wear the leaves. They're waterproof. They get rained on all the time, don't they?"

"Oh, Roob," she swoons. "You're so smart."

I blush. "Thanks."

"Is there something wrong?" she asks. "You look worried."

"Just thinking about a friend and his father," I tell her.

"Is there anything I can do?"

I shake my head. "I don't want to worry about it right now. All I want is for you to be my girlfriend."

"I'm still not sure," she answers.

"What's wrong with me?"

"Nothing. It's just that I don't know you."

A loud roar thunders down the beach.

"Roob!" Rachel screams. "Look over there! What on earth is that horrible thing?"

I stare in horror at the monster charging toward us. "I think it's . . ."

* * *

"Mind if we share the table?" A large woman with a tray-ful of tacos loomed over me. Two snotty little kids were buzzing around her legs. "All the tables are full," she told me. "Mind if we share yours?"

I stood up. "I was just leaving anyway."

I wanted to wait until things were less crowded around the Burger Baron. Besides, I needed more time to work up my courage. I couldn't just walk up to Rachel and say, "I'll have a cheeseburger. Hold the onions." That was too normal. I needed to make my small talk special. More snappy. More witty.

I began to walk down the mall. How about, "Cheeseburger please. No onions. Gosh, you're gorgeous. Do you want to join the astronaut training program with me? We could blast into outer space. I'd love to be weightless with you."

Dumb.

What about, "I believe I'll have a cheeseburger with no onions. Aren't you the girl who won the Ms Teeny-Wonderful contest I saw on TV for the most beautiful, talented, charming girl in the universe?"

No, she'd know I was laying it on thick.

Course, I could be brutal and say, "Wow, I recognize you from school. I'll have a cheeseburger with no onions. I love you, and even though I'm only in eighth grade, I want to spend the rest of eternity on a deserted island with you.

Several people gave me strange looks when I started laughing to myself.

Still undecided about what to say, I detoured into the bookstore.

I spent the next fifteen minutes in the health section browsing through the sex books. Finding none with

decent pictures, I strolled over to the books for young
people and checked out Dad's shelf.

His books were all there, the *Boy Scout Buddies*, the
Baby-Watchers Gang and the *Junior Romance Novels for
Boys*. I picked up a new *Boy Scout* book, one I hadn't
seen before. Above Dad's name on the cover were the
words "created by." I wondered what that meant.

I checked the latest in the *Baby-Watchers* and *Romance* series. The same words appeared above his name
on those books too.

"Created by," I muttered. "Guess that's the new way
of saying 'written by.'"

Two elementary school girls wandered by. They were
saying how disappointed they were the store didn't have
the latest *Baby-Watchers Gang Super Special*.

I told them it was one of my father's books and that
he'd be visiting me soon and I was going to live with him
in a trailer. They looked at me like I was some kind of
junior-high sex pervert and left real quick.

"Oh, well," I whispered to myself. "It's now or never.
Let's go order a hamburger."

* * *

By the time I returned to the Burger Baron, the crowd
had thinned. Only two customers hid Rachel Parsons
from my sight. I rolled up the sleeves of my jacket so I
looked cool, took a deep breath to kill the flutterbys in
my stomach, combed my hair with my fingers and
walked up to the counter.

The customers left as I arrived. So there I was, face to
face, with . . . with. . . . Who the heck was this?

A plump, middle-aged woman wearing a dopey purple
vest and paper crown smiled at me. "What would you
like?"

For a moment I was speechless. I expected to see Five-Freckles-on-Her-Nose.

"Yes?" the woman asked.

"Cheeseburger. No onions."

She punched my order into the cash register.

"Fries?"

I nodded.

"Soft drink?"

"Diet Coke. Excuse me, what happened to the girl who was working here about twenty minutes ago?"

The woman placed a paper bag on the counter. "You mean Rachel?"

"Is she still around?"

The woman filled my order from the warming trays, packing the bag. "Rachel's gone."

"Gone?" I had the horrible thought she'd suffered some kind of terrible accident. Maybe part of her body had got caught in the bun toaster or something.

"She only works until one-thirty," the woman told me as she poured the Diet Coke. "I think she said she had cheerleading practice this afternoon."

I breathed a sigh of relief. Rachel Parsons was still in one piece.

The woman threw a couple of ketchup packets in the bag. "Five-fifty, please."

* * *

I sat at a table, too disappointed to eat. Now I was going to have to wait another whole week before I spoke to Rachel.

I didn't get to dwell on my misery for long. "I want to talk to you, Roob," someone said.

I focused on the face of Robert Lopez. "I want to talk to you about something important."

7

BOOB, ROOB AND POMPOMS

*B*ob slid into the bench opposite me. He looked the perfect jock, muscles bulging under his T-shirt, Walkman earphones dangling around his neck, fake gold chain glistening just below his Adam's apple. "We have to talk."

"No, we don't," I answered. "Please go away. I'm in the middle of feeling sorry for myself."

He ignored my comment. "I've been doing a lot of thinking since yesterday," he began.

"Go chase cars or something," I said. "I'm in mourning."

Again, he ignored me. "It's not just me. It's James and John Price too. We've been thinking we're not exactly thrilled you're on the track team."

"Neither am I," I told him. "But what the heck. That's life, right? Now, just go away and let me be miserable by myself."

"I think Mr. Simpson is making a big mistake letting you on the team," he went on. "Everybody knows you're one big flake."

"A flake? I'm a piece of cereal?"

"It means you're strange," he explained.

"You're starting to bother me," I insisted. "I really need

to be alone. Find something else to do. Go to the zoo and scare the animals or something."

"Listen, Roob. I want you to know that the track team is important to me. I think we have a chance of doing real great this year. I don't want you to mess things up."

I wasn't up for this. Why wouldn't he go away? I cupped my hand around my ear. "Hark, I hear the mating call of a female moose. That means you have to go right away, right?"

Lopez stared at me for a few seconds. "You know, you're not a flake. You're crazy. I think they should lock you up somewhere."

"The same place you escaped from?"

"Don't make me angry, Fowler."

I laughed. "Okay, Boob."

Back in fifth grade, our teacher used to call me Rob and Lopez, Bob, to avoid confusion. When everyone started calling me Roob, it was natural for me to call Lopez, Boob. He hated it and beat the crapola out of me to make me stop. I knew it was dumb to use it now, but missing Rachel had really upset me. I was in a stupid mood.

"Don't call me that," he said.

"Why not? It suits you. Boob, Boob, Boob, Boob."

Whenever Lopez gets mad, red blotches appear all over his neck.

"Shut up, Fowler!"

I watched pink splotches blossom around his Adam's apple. "Boob, Boob, Boob, Boob."

He stood up and raised his fist, ready to plant knuckles into my teeth. I stood too and pointed over his shoulder. "Watch out, Rent-a-cop," I said.

Lopez twisted around to look for the security guard. Of course, there was nobody there. By the time he turned back to me, I had a ketchup packet a hands-length from his face. I crushed one end, exploding the other. A spray of Heinz splashed a flower shape over his nose and forehead.

"Every hot dog needs a little ketchup," I taunted.

Then I decided it was in my best interest to vanish. As he swore and wiped his eyes, I darted away.

* * *

When I opened the back door, I found Mom mopping the kitchen floor. Instead of "Hi, Rob," I got a faceful of "Sit down!"

I slumped in a chair. I didn't have a clue what was bugging her this time. But I did know I didn't have the patience for another of her lectures. After Paul's dad, missing Rachel, and Robert Lopez, I was ready to argue back.

Mom rested the mop in the pail and stood over me with her hands on her hips. "I'm disgusted by the state of your room. If I'd known it was such a mess, I wouldn't have let you leave this house."

So that was it. My room? Of all the stupid things to get mad about. "You made me clean it a couple of weeks ago. It can't be that bad."

"There are dirty clothes all over the floor," Mom complained. "The sheets should have been changed last weekend. I found chip bags and a chocolate-bar wrapper under the bed."

There was one logical way to solve this problem. "If you don't like it, don't go in. I always close my door."

"That's not good enough. I want this house kept clean."

So much for logic. I tried the truth. "You know what, Mom? I think you're neurotic about being clean. I think you should get some help. So what if things are a little messy? It's no big deal. Normal people don't clean the bathtub everyday. Normal people don't vacuum the floors every night. Normal people wear clothes two days in a row. Normal people don't run around the house dusting picture frames. Normal people don't mop the floors twice a week. You're not normal, Mom."

"You will not talk to me that way!" she shouted. "I'm your mother and I deserve respect."

"Give me a break."

Then she reached for something on the counter and threw it on the table. "Explain why you brought this trash into my home."

It was an old copy of *Playboy* I'd bought in the second-hand book store. "How'd you find that? I kept it under the mattress. You've been snooping around, haven't you?"

"Just answer my question," she yelled. "Why do you have this garbage?"

"Get out of my face."

"Why is it in my house?"

"Because I'm interested in the pictures!" I yelled back. "And it's none of your business anyway. You have no right poking around my room."

"I have every right. I'm your mother."

"And I wish you weren't," I shot back.

"Get out!" she screamed. "Get out of this house!"

"Gladly." I stood up and opened the door. "Anything to get away from you."

I don't think I've ever seen Mom angrier than she was at that moment, and I can remember the doozy fights she used to have with Dad before they split. Veins bulged across her forehead, and she clenched her teeth so hard the tendons danced in her neck. I didn't want to wait around to see what would happen next.

* * *

I spent the next hour meandering around the neighborhood. At first I tried to figure out what had just happened between Mom and me. I didn't understand it. How had we got to the point of being at each other's throats all the time? Nothing was right anymore.

It wasn't just Mom I didn't understand. I tried to figure

why I was goofing around at school. Why I didn't care about anything that went on at Maid of the Mist. And why Paul was so messed up. Everything was so confusing.

So, I thought about something more pleasant.

* * *

"What is that?" Rachel screams. "What is that horrible-looking monster running toward us?"

I step in front of her to protect her. "Holy moly," I gasp. "That's an Albertosaurus. It's a dinosaur from the Cretaceous Period, about one hundred million years ago. It's a giant flesh eater. Note its powerful hind legs and its tiny forearms. Note its gigantic claws and huge teeth for grabbing and tearing its prey. It was thought to be extinct, but obviously this island has somehow escaped the passage of time. Albertosauruses have survived here."

Rachel ooohs. "Ooh, Roob. You're so smart."

I grin, delighted by the praise. "Thank you."

"Is it dangerous?" Rachel asks.

"Would you consider a flesh-eating monster that weighs as much as a bus and has over one hundred razor-sharp, fifteen-centimeter-long teeth dangerous?"

"Yes," she answers.

"My guess too."

"Ooh, Roob. What are we going to do? I'm too young to be eaten by an Albertosa . . . Albertose . . . Albertoso . . ."

"Albertosaurus."

"Thank you. I'm too young to be eaten by one of those."

The monster opens it jaws and howls a spine-chilling cry into the sky. Its claws plow into the beach, dislodging truckloads of sand. Saliva oozes between its killer teeth and drips like clear honey off its chin.

"Fear not," I proclaim bravely. "Yonder beast will not harm a hair on your brown, curly head or a freckle on your freckled nose. I will protect you."

"Ooh, Roob," she says. "What are you going to do? Will you jump bravely onto its scaly back and choke it to death? Will you climb that palm tree and throw a ripe, juicy coconut at its head? Will you let it eat you, so it will forget all about me?"

I shake my head. "No, my dear. I have a better plan."

"And what is that?" she wonders.

"Run for your life!" I holler.

I grab her hand and pull. We race madly across the beach. Me and Rachel Parsons, holding hands, running away from a charging dinosaur . . .

* * *

Now, that's a real romance story, I thought. That's the stuff Dad should be writing. That's what true love is all about.

I checked my watch. Almost three. Time for track team practice, time to sprain my ankle and drop out of the team.

It was a scummy thing I was about to do. All of a sudden, it seemed like a completely bogus idea. Sure it would help Paul, but it would certainly disappoint Mr. Simpson. He thought I was going to help the team.

When I got to the school I saw the cheerleaders by the bleachers. There sure were a lot of keeners at Maid of the Mist Middle School gung-ho about Saturday practices. Then I remembered what the woman in the Burger Baron had said. "I think she said she has cheerleading practice this afternoon."

I quickly scanned the group of girls and, there she was. Rachel Parsons stood holding her pompoms in one hand and adjusting her teeny, tiny skirt with the other.

I walked over to the bleachers and sat in the first row. A dozen other spectators, parents and boyfriends, were already watching the practice. Ms. Gomez, the girls' gym teacher, gave me an absent glance for a moment before returning her attention to the girls.

The next ten minutes were among the happiest of my entire life. I was transfixed on the jumping, bouncing form of the world's greatest cheerleader. Nobody could possibly do better high leg kicks than Rachel Parsons. Nobody could wave pompoms like that. Nobody, anywhere, could shout, "Go, team, go" in the same moving way.

Heaven has got to be like this, I thought.

"Rob!" Mr. Simpson called. "Rob Fowler. Let's go!"

I was forced to divert my eyes from Rachel to my gym teacher. Mr. Simpson was standing in an open doorway of the school, waving me over. "Get in here."

I sighed. So much for my taste of heaven. Reluctantly, I hopped down and jogged across the field.

Mr. Simpson pointed to his watch as I walked into the school. "You're late, Robert. I was starting to wonder if you'd forgotten or changed your mind." Then he tousled my hair, like I was a little kid. "Glad you're here. Now my team is together."

"Yes, sir," I mumbled.

"You need a haircut," Mr. Simpson said. "Get one as soon as possible. Too much hair means wind resistance. Go get changed."

"Yes, sir."

I grabbed my gym bag from my locker and strolled to the change room with images of Rachel Parsons bouncing in my head. I should have been thinking about my teammates and about who one of them was, the one I'd painted with ketchup at lunchtime. Bob Lopez took me completely by surprise.

8

THE RACE

As soon as I entered the locker room, Lopez flew at me. He thudded his shoulder into my chest, bashing me against the lockers. I groaned and tried to suck back my breath.

Lopez didn't let up. He pummelled my head with his right fist. Smack. Smack. Punches bounced off my temple. A claw of pain shot down my face. Smack. Another swing cuffed my ear. My head started ringing like a fire alarm and tiny, white novas flashed before my eyes.

Then Lopez shoved his left fist into my gut. I groaned again. If I'd eaten lunch, I'd have lost it.

Smack. Another blow to my temple. I didn't have the strength to fight back. I was wobbly and dizzy and hurting.

Through blurry eyes, I saw Paul grab Lopez and yank him backwards. There was a lot of shouting, but I wasn't sure if it was Paul or Lopez or me. When my head cleared, I saw that James Price and Paul had wrapped my furious attacker in a bear hug.

Bob couldn't move. So I shoved my fist into his face. The punch wasn't that hard because I was still groggy, but I was pleased to see a trickle of blood roll lazily down his upper lip.

"What did you do that for!" Paul yelled.

The change-room door burst open and Mr. Simpson charged in. He looked at Lopez's bloody nose. Then he looked at me. "What on earth is going on here?"

* * *

A few minutes later, Robert Lopez and I were shaking hands.

I discovered Mr. Simpson wants a number-one track team real bad. So bad he didn't dump on me at all.

Lopez's nose stopped bleeding pretty fast. My head and gut were sore, but I recovered quickly too. After Bob washed his face, Mr. Simpson made us sit on a change-room bench.

"Listen, boys," he began. "I'm not sure what this is all about and, frankly, I don't care. I just don't want it to happen again. You two are on the same team for the next month. Whatever the problem is between you, it doesn't exist until track season is over. Got it?"

Lopez grunted an "uh-huh" and I nodded.

"Shake hands," Mr. Simpson ordered.

Lopez held out his hand and I shook it. "Sorry," he muttered. "I owed you for the ketchup. You're my teammate."

"Good," the coach declared. "Good. Now get outside and start jogging around the track."

* * *

"I can't believe it," Paul said as we jogged side by side. "I can't believe you hit Bob while Price was holding him."

I watched Lopez and the Price twins jogging ten meters in front of us. "What's there not to believe?" I said. "He punched me around."

"It wasn't fair," Paul said, panting. "Bob couldn't defend himself."

"Don't be dorky. *It wasn't fair*," I mocked. "Get serious."

"I just didn't think you could do something like that," Paul said as we passed the bleachers.

I hoped Rachel Parsons would watch me trot gracefully by. No such luck. None of the cheerleaders bothered to look at us.

"You're so different now," Paul went on.

"You sound like my mother."

"It's true. You have a different attitude toward everything."

"Such as?" I wanted to know.

"Such as the track team," he said. "I remember you telling me in sixth grade that you wanted to be on the track team. Now it's just an excuse to impress Mrs. Druchek."

"I've been thinking about that," I told him. "Mr. Simpson really thinks I'm going to help the team. It won't be fair if I fake an injury."

"Hey, don't change your mind on me," Paul said, worried. "You're doing it to help me, remember?"

"I'm not the only one who's changed. You wouldn't have let me do it last year. You would have wanted to make the team fair and square."

"I know, Roob. Ever since I started eighth grade, everything has got so serious."

"Some things," I agreed.

"The things I used to think when I was a little kid seem stupid all of a sudden," Paul said. "My father has made me understand that winning isn't everything, it's the only thing. I have to be top student. I have to make the track team. No matter what it costs."

I resisted the urge to tell him about his father's bribe. It wouldn't help anything.

"Sometimes when my dad is pushing me, making me study all the time, wanting me to make the track team so bad, it all seems too much, and I feel like I'm going to explode."

"I feel the same way when Mom is bugging me."

"This is more than just being bugged," he said. "It makes me want to hang off a bridge."

My heart did a lurch. "You definitely should talk to Mr. Welles. That's what he's there for."

We passed the bleachers again. Again, Rachel wasn't watching.

"I have to retie my shoes," Paul said. "I'll catch you next lap." He veered toward the seats.

That left me alone with my imagination.

* * *

"You're running too fast, Roob," Rachel cries. "I can't keep up with you."

"I'm on the Maid of the Mist track team," I point out. "I'm a natural runner. I'll slow down a little for you. But not too slow. Remember what's chasing us."

The Albertosaurus roars in anger, frustrated that we are fleeing so quickly. Its hunger drives it wild and it turns on the speed. The ground shakes under the footsteps of the terrible, thundering lizard.

"It's getting closer," Rachel yells. "I don't want to be eaten by such a horrible beast."

"Have no fear," I yell. "Everything is under control. Quick, into the opening of this cave, which is large enough for us to enter, but way too small for that lumbering giant."

We dive into the cave mere seconds before the monster catches us. It howls and thrusts its massive head at the too-small entrance, exhaling foul carnivore breath over us. We scramble backwards until we fall onto the chairs.

"That was close," Rachel notes as the Albertosaurus thumps outside the cave.

"Chairs?" I wonder. "We're sitting on chairs. Chairs in a cave on a deserted island?"

As our eyes adjust to the semi-darkness, we notice the cave is full of furniture. Furniture made of crude, rough wood, tied together with vines, but perfect for a cave on a deserted island. There's two chairs, a table, shelves and a bed covered with a reed mattress.

"Do you think anyone lives here?" Rachel asks.

I wipe my hand across a tabletop. My fingers are covered in dust. "Not recently," I answer.

"I wonder who it was?" Rachel says.

I read the carvings on the tabletop. "Robinson Crusoe was here."

"Wow!"

The dinosaur still thrashes outside, bellowing in fury.

"I don't think we should go outside tonight," I say. "It will be too dangerous."

Rachel glances around the room. "You mean you and I are going to spend a whole night in here alone?"

I grin and nod.

"But that's not right."

"What's wrong with it?"

"Well, for one thing, there's only one bed."

"It's no problem," I say. "We could simply . . ."

* * *

Mr. Simpson's whistle broke my concentration. My teammates stood next to him by the bleachers. "Let's go, Robert," he called.

As I jogged up to them, I noticed Ms. Gomez breaking up the cheerleader practice.

"Okay," the coach said. "I assume you're warmed up now. Let's have a little race and see who's the fastest. Let's see who's going to be the finisher, the main man of our team."

"We already decided that, Coach," James Price said. "There's no way John, Paul or I can beat Bob."

Mr. Simpson pointed at me. "That was before Robert volunteered to join us."

I smiled at the word *volunteered.*

"There's no way Roob can beat Bob," James pointed out.

Mr. Simpson scratched his gut. "Why don't we wait and see? I want you to race to the hundred-meter mark." He turned to the disbanding cheerleaders. "Excuse me, girls. Would one of you volunteer to be a judge for us? It'll only take a minute."

Rachel Parsons bobbed out of the group. "I will," she said. "What would you like me to do?"

"The boys are going to race," Mr. Simpson explained. "Would you mind going to the hundred-meter mark and watching who finishes first?"

She fluffed her curls and handed her pompoms to Mr. Simpson. "Okay, will you hold these for me?" Then she jogged down the track to the finish line.

"You look cute with those, sir," James Price noted.

"How come I never get to hold pompoms?" John Price asked.

I wished I was holding Rachel's pompoms for her. I wouldn't feel silly.

"Keep your minds on the race, gentlemen," Mr. Simpson warned. "Pick a lane."

We shuffled across the track and spread out. James Price took the inside lane. His brother took the second. Bob Lopez was in the third lane. Then me. Then Paul.

"On your marks."

We squatted into a four-point sprinter's stance.

Lopez twisted his head and taunted me. "I'm going to run so fast, the only thing you'll see is my tail feathers."

I didn't bother to respond. I was watching Rachel Parsons. She reached the hundred-meter mark, turned around and waved to Mr. Simpson to let us know she was ready.

"Get set!"

"Good luck with your injury," Paul whispered.

Rachel Parsons was going to watch me race. In a moment, I would get a chance to show off in front of the world's greatest cheerleader. What an opportunity. When Rachel saw me blaze in front of everybody, she'd be duly and incredibly impressed.

"Go!" Mr. Simpson shouted.

The Prices, Lopez and Paul exploded into a full run. I was concentrating so much on Rachel it took me a moment to realize I was supposed to be running too. I pushed off, meters behind them.

I leaned forward, swinging my arms in tense thrusts. I dug my Reeboks into the cinder, forcing my leg muscles to discharge all the strength I had.

I passed the Prices and Paul at the same time.

With every stride, my feet thudded the ground and my hair bounced on my head, making popping sounds against my ears.

But I wasn't gaining on Lopez. He cranked on like a machine. I had the image of Arnold Schwarzenegger running in the old Terminator movies. Left. Right. Left. Right. Perfect motion. I couldn't catch him.

I saw Rachel at the finish line. She vibrated in my vision as I tried to catch the cyborg in front of me.

"Come on, Roob," my mind was coaching. "Rachel is watching. You can't lose in front of Rachel Parsons.

For some crazy reason the little kid's story about the red engine and the hill flashed through my mind. The one where it makes it by saying, "I think I can. I think I can."

I swung my arms wider, almost like I was swimming, hoping it would somehow propel me faster.

It worked. I was gaining on Lopez. I was closing the gap so fast . . . I could have caught him easily if we hadn't crossed the finish line when we did.

Bob Lopez passed the hundred-meter mark a length in front of me.

As I slowed to a stop I saw Rachel point at Bob. "He won," she called to Mr. Simpson. Then she pointed at me. "Roob was a close second."

Roob? I wondered. Rachel knows my name? How could she know my name?

"A close race," a voice added behind me. "Real close."

I knew the voice. The last time I'd heard it was on the phone a month ago. I twisted around.

Dad stood grinning at me. "So how's my kid?" he asked.

9

So Erudite

I must have been grinning like a happy face because my cheeks actually hurt. I rushed over and threw my arms around Dad. "I'm so glad you got here."

He didn't return the hug. Instead he gently pushed me away. I noticed the smell of beer on his breath.

"I'm happy to see you too." Dad took a step back and looked me up and down. "Wow, big changes. You're almost as tall as me."

He'd changed too. His ponytail was longer and he'd grown a beard. I was surprised at how many gray whiskers he had. Also, he'd gained about ten pounds, maybe more. A handle of paunch rolled over his belt buckle.

"How did you know I was here?"

"I dropped by the house. Your mother told me you were probably at track practice."

"Is Mom still mad at me?"

"Mad may be too nice a word. She is one angry human being."

"Mom and I have . . ." I stopped when I noticed Dad was staring over my shoulder.

I turned around and saw Paul, James and John Price, Lopez and Rachel watching us. Mr. Simpson, the pompoms bouncing in his hands, jogged past them. He stopped, appeared suddenly embarrassed, backstepped and handed the pompoms back to Rachel. Then he walked over to us.

"Sig Simpson," the coach announced as he shook Dad's hand. "I'm Robert's gym teacher and track coach."

"Stephen Fowler," Dad introduced himself.

"I know who you are," Mr. Simpson replied. "I've never met a famous author before. It's an honor meeting you."

Dad smiled. "Yeah, it is, isn't it? I'd be honored to meet me too."

Mr. Simpson seemed unsure what to say next. "I beg your pardon?"

Dad laughed. "I always say that. I like to see the strange looks on people's faces. I'm just kidding."

"Oh."

"So how's Rob doing?" Dad asked. "That was one mean run, wasn't it?"

Mr. Simpson agreed. "It *was* a great run, Robert," he said to me. "If you'd had a better start, it would have been a lot closer. You really put on the burners near the finish."

I glanced over at Rachel. When she saw me looking at her, she broke into a wide smile.

My insides boiled into mush. *The* Rachel Parsons was actually looking at *me* and smiling.

"Robert is a natural runner," Mr. Simpson told Dad. "With him on the track team, I'm sure we'll do well. We're . . ."

"That's nice," Dad interrupted. "Look, Mr. Samson, no offense, but I'm really not interested in the track team."

The coach bristled. "I thought you'd be interested because Robert was on the team."

Dad shook his head. "Not at all. I'm going to take Rob with me now."

I could tell Mr. Simpson was miffed. "We've only just

started our practice," he said. "We need to work on baton passing. I'm sure Robert would be proud if you decided to watch."

My father shook his head. "No thanks. Rob's coming with me now."

"I understand," Mr. Simpson said, although his tone made sure we knew he didn't.

"Good. Go get changed, Rob. I'll be waiting in the truck." Dad waved to Paul and shouted, "Good to see you, Paul." Then he shook my teacher's hand again. "Nice meeting you, Mr. Samson."

I figured the coach would correct him this time, but he didn't. "You too, Mr. Fowler," Mr. Simpson said dryly.

Dad started walking to his truck. "Hurry up, Rob," he ordered.

* * *

I changed in less than a minute. I couldn't believe my incredible good fortune. Dad was here. Rachel Parsons had smiled at me. What a terrific day. My luck had changed, just like that.

The only thing that worried me was Dad's breath. He had promised he'd never drink again. Then I thought I had it figured. There was that non-alcohol beer. Dad had probably had one of those.

I threw my strip in my locker and charged out the door. Across the parking lot, I noticed my track teammates practicing with the baton. I couldn't see Rachel anywhere. She'd probably gone home.

When I pulled open the door to Dad's Cherokee, I almost died. I felt the blood drain from my face; a nauseating heave pulsed through my intestines. I couldn't believe what I saw.

Rachel Parsons was sitting in the back seat of Dad's truck.

"Hi, Roob," she said. "My name's Rachel."

"Ba . . ." A noose of nerves tightened my throat.

"You probably don't know me, but I feel like I know you," Rachel went on. "Ever since someone told me you were Stephen Fowler's son, I've wanted to talk to you. I just love your father's books."

"Wa . . ."

"Rachel came over and asked for my autograph," Dad explained. "I gave her one of my new *Baby-Watcher's Gang* books. I also offered her a ride home. I always offer a pretty girl a ride home."

Rachel blushed slightly.

"Well, don't stand there looking like an extra in *Night of the Living Dead*," Dad teased. "Get in, Rob."

Rachel lives three blocks from the school. It took us a minute to drive to her house. She told Dad how much she enjoyed the *Baby-Watcher's Gang* series. He told her about the next two novels, which would be out this fall. And I said nothing.

The whole time, I said absolutely nothing. I didn't turn around to look at Rachel. I just stared at the glove compartment. Rachel Parsons was in my father's truck, so close I could touch her, and I was acting like a zombie.

"Thanks for giving me the book, Mr. Fowler," Rachel said when we pulled into her driveway. "And thanks for signing it." She opened the truck door. "Say, Mr. Fowler, how come it has 'created by' next to your name? Does that mean you didn't write it?"

"My name is on the book, isn't it?" Dad replied.

Rachel closed the door, then walked up to my window. "Now that we know each other, Roob, maybe we can eat lunch together or something?"

"Da . . ." I answered.

"I'll save a chair for you in the cafeteria on Monday." She bounced into her house.

Dad stared at me, a half-grin on his face. "No doubt you impressed her with your conversation. It was so erudite."

"What?"

"It means you showed off your great intelligence and education."

I felt like I wanted to melt into the leather seats.

"You like her, *Roob*?" He said *Roob* in an imitation of Rachel's voice.

"I think I'm in love with her, Dad."

He chuckled. "Love? I was in *love* with a different girl every week when I was your age."

"This is the real thing," I said. "I've been thinking about her for two months. I imagine I'm stuck on a deserted island with her."

Dad backed the Cherokee into the road. "And what are you and Rachel doing on this island?"

"Nothing much. Running away from dinosaurs, hiding in Robinson Crusoe's cave and stuff." All of a sudden, I felt dumb revealing my daydream. First, Dad had seen me tongue-tied by a girl. Next I confess to a dopey imagination. "You were kind of hard on Mr. Simpson. You kept calling him Mr. Samson," I said to change the subject.

"Oh, yeah?" He acted surprised by my statement. "I didn't mean to be rude. Your coach is a bit of a door knob. People like that bother me. What are you doing on the track team anyway?"

I told Dad the truth. About being a skin layer away from being expelled. How I had to suck up so I wouldn't get kicked out and have Mom pull a total hairy. How I planned to fake a sprained ankle so I could quit and still win the suck-up points.

"I don't know why you're worrying about your mom having a fit. She's done that already. What did you do to upset her today? I asked and she said she didn't want to discuss it because it would only make her angry."

"My room was dirty."

"Oh, that. She's still at the cleaning thing, is she?"

"She's nuts about it, Dad."

"I know. I was married to her for almost ten years. I don't know how I stood it. Stupid woman."

I didn't like the way he said that. I didn't like him calling Mom stupid. He shouldn't talk about Mom that way.

Then I remembered what Mom had said during our argument earlier. She said *I* didn't have any respect for her.

"Why are you looking like that?" Dad asked.

"No reason."

"Look, Rob, before I forget, the next time we meet, no hugs, okay? Guys don't hug."

"You used to hug me when I was little."

"That's different. Let's go to Glowing Embers," he suggested. "Let's go to my trailer and we can talk."

* * *

Glowing Embers is an RV park on Grand Island, the big island that splits the Niagara River on the American side. The owners think it's neat to have someone famous stay there, so they give Dad a big discount on his campsite rent.

Dad's trailer is a 17-footer, pretty cramped space for a kitchen, living room, bedroom and bathroom. But it's loaded with goodies — roof air conditioner, color TV, microwave, bath and shower, everything.

The first thing Dad did after opening the trailer door was grab a couple of cans of Miller from the fridge. "I think you're old enough to have a brewski with your old man. I promise I won't tell your mother."

"No, thanks," I said.

"When I was your age I used to sneak a beer or two off Grandpa," Dad bragged. "He never even knew they were missing."

I only have vague memories of Dad's father since he

died of a heart attack when I was only five. Mom said he was a heavy drinker.

"I don't like the taste," I said.

Dad replaced the beer with a can of Diet Coke and tossed it to me. We sat on the couch. Dad pulled the tab and took a long swallow.

"How come you're still drinking?" I demanded. "You swore you'd never drink again. You promised me last year."

He chuckled. "I did stop drinking. This is beer. Beer is not drinking."

"It has alcohol in it," I pointed out.

"A little bit," he agreed. "Not enough to give me a buzz. I drink it because I like the taste. You can't get drunk on beer."

"That's not true," I argued. "I've seen the high-school kids at the park. They get loaded on beer. In Health, Mr. Simpson told us a beer has as much alcohol as a shot of whiskey."

"Talking about this is silly." Dad sounded annoyed. "When I was an alcoholic, I used to drink a bottle of Scotch a day. Now I have a couple of beers. It's not the same thing. Tell me about you. You're having a hard time with your mom and at school?"

"Yeah." I took a sip of cola.

"It's a normal part of growing up. Don't get out of whack about it. Remember, it'll seem stupid in a couple of years." He finished the beer with another gulp, tossed the can into the garbage and got up to get another.

"You can recycle those," I told him.

"I don't have to do that stuff." He laughed. "I'm Stephen Fowler and I can do anything I want."

I laughed too, even though it wasn't funny.

"Paul looks so different," Dad said. "What's the matter with him? He looks like he has a loaded A-bomb in his shorts. You still friends with him?"

"Yeah, but we're not as close as we used to be."

Then I told Dad about what happened on the bridge over on Goat Island. I expected him to give me some advice, tell me what to do to help Paul. Instead he took another gulp of beer. "Psycho-boy," he observed. "Stay away from the looney-tunes. They'll suck you into cartoon-land."

"I'd like to help him," I said.

Dad answered with a belch. "Keeps the mice away." He laughed again. "Let's watch some TV. Glowing Embers has cable hook-up this year. There's got to be a basketball game on." He picked up the remote and fired up the set.

"Before we do that, can I ask you something important?" I wanted to talk about the idea of my living with him. "When you and Mom split, you agreed . . ."

"Let's talk about it later," he said. "It's the Lakers and Celtics. You still love b-ball?"

"Sure, I . . ."

"What a shot. You see that?"

I guessed it would have to wait. All of a sudden I felt depressed.

10

DAD

*E*very time there was a break in the game, I told Dad some of the things that had happened at school . . . the frog in Science, the volleyball in Mr. Simpson's gut, the fire in Home Ec, and so on. Dad kind of listened, answering either with a grunt or "That's my boy."

It soon became obvious to me that Dad's definition of "a couple of beers" meant a lot more than two. The pop of a fresh beer can became a familiar sound.

When he wasn't watching the game or visiting the fridge, Dad described some of the places he'd been during the winter and some of the people he'd met, but not in detail.

Once he asked about Helen. When I told him she was practically living with Woody the basketball player, he didn't seem all that interested.

"Basketball? At least he's playing the right sport. Is this Woody an okay guy?"

"I've only met him a couple of times. He seems really moody. I don't think Mom likes it that Helen's seeing him."

Dad didn't seem worried. "Your sister has always been able to take care of herself."

I was surprised when Dad told me he'd arrived at Glowing Embers on Thursday night.

"Thursday? That was two days ago. How come you didn't come over to visit us then?"

"Got in real late."

"What happened yesterday?" I wanted to know.

"I slept in," he answered. "In the afternoon, I met this couple, the Bakers, from Nevada. We had a couple of beers and started talking about the best places to camp around Pyramid Lake. You remember I stayed there two years ago. The day was shot. I'll introduce you to them tomorrow. They're camped by the river."

That hurt. "Isn't seeing your kids more important than drinking beer with strangers?"

Dad missed the sarcasm. "You know I go with the flow. What's the problem? We're together now."

"The problem is, I haven't seen you in a year."

"So what difference is another day?" Dad said, flicking the remote. "That was a good game. You want some supper?"

"Sure. What do you have?"

"Nothing. I gave up cooking," he announced proudly. "Cooking is for people who don't have something more important to do. Let's go out."

"I don't know," I hedged.

"What's up?" Dad asked.

"It's just that . . . it's just . . ."

"What?"

"You've had a lot of beer. Maybe you shouldn't drive anywhere."

Dad stared at me like I'd just told him I was the ghost of Elvis. "You've been counting how many beers I've had?"

"I noticed, that's all," I said sheepishly. "You got up six times."

"So what? Do I sound drunk? Do I look drunk? It's just beer, Rob. I told you, beer doesn't affect me at all."

"But, you're . . ."

"I don't want to hear any more garbage about how many beers I drink."

"I thought . . ."

"Don't think." His frown smoothed. "I'm cool, Rob. I'm always cool. Don't worry about me. Let's go to a restaurant."

* * *

Maybe I overreacted. Dad drove into Niagara Falls with no problem. I was really paranoid though, expecting him to drive through a red light or something, but he seemed normal.

He continued to drink in the restaurant, having a couple of glasses of wine with dinner.

"Don't look at me like that, Rob," he said. "You know I always have a glass of wine with supper. I enjoy my meal better with a glass of wine. I'm going to get angry if you start hassling me about what I eat too."

So I bit my tongue, feeling more upset by the minute.

"When I was your age I was so dumb," Dad told me between mouthfuls of steak. "I was living in Toronto then. Right downtown. We had a neighborhood gang called the Black Angels. Have I ever told you this?"

"A few times."

"We used to fight with the guys in the next school. They called themselves the Hell Cats. Stupid, huh?"

"Yeah."

"You sure I've told you this before?"

"You used to rumble behind the supermarket parking lot. Some store called Dominion. I've heard it all before, Dad."

"Did I ever tell you about my girlfriend?"

"Elaine," I recited. "Long, dark hair and super-cute."

Now that I thought about it, Dad always told me his "way back when" stories after he'd had a few drinks.

"She looked a little like the one we gave a ride to this afternoon. Only cuter. Wonder what ever happened to her?"

I couldn't imagine anybody cuter than Rachel Parsons. It just wasn't possible.

"Dad, I want to ask you something important."

"I need a potty break first," Dad announced. He put his knife and fork on the plate, stood up and called to the waitress. "I'll have another glass of wine over here. You need another milk, Rob?"

I shook my head.

The waitress brought the wine while Dad was in the can. When he returned to the table, he downed half the glass and said, "So tell me what's so important?"

"I've been doing a lot of thinking lately. You know, about Mom and school and stuff like that."

"And?"

"I think I want to live with you."

He picked his teeth with a fingernail for a few moments, not saying anything. Finally, "You want to live with me? Like in my trailer, all the time?"

"Remember when you and Mom split up, you said when I was old enough to choose, I could make up my own mind. I think I'm old enough now."

He continued to pick his teeth.

"I'll sleep on the couch," I went on. "I won't get into any trouble."

Dad took another healthy gulp of vino. "Why do you want to live with me?"

"Because I'm not happy here," I explained. "Nobody understands me in Niagara Falls. Mom doesn't. My teachers don't. I think I'll be happier with you."

"Me and my kid. Might be fun."

"Yeah!" I punched my fist into the air. "That's terrific. This is going to make everything okay."

Dad leaned back in his chair. "Whoa, I didn't say yes yet.

I'll have to think about it, Rob. It would be a pretty big step for me. I'm kind of used to being a loner. I'm not sure I want a kid around."

"I'm not just a kid," I defended. "I'm your son."

"You know what I mean. And what about school?"

"I've already thought of that. I'll do my lessons through the mail. Correspondence courses."

Dad shook his head. "I don't know. The trailer's too small for the two of us. One night is okay. Every night, we'd drive each other nuts. Besides you'd cramp my style."

"I wouldn't bug you when you're writing," I repeated.

Dad looked strangely embarrassed when I said that.

Then I remembered Rachel's question. "How come all your new books say *created by*?"

He finished his wine and stared into the empty glass.

"Is that the same as *written by*?" I wanted to know.

He looked up at me, and for the first time in my entire life I saw a look on my father's face that frightened me. He looked ashamed, like a little kid who'd been caught with both hands and both feet in the cookie jar.

"What's wrong, Dad? Are you okay?"

"I have a little confession to make, Rob," he said softly. "I've been going through a dry spell with my writing in the last year. Maybe a little longer than that. In fact, I haven't written a novel in over two years."

"How can that be? There's a couple of new *Baby-Watchers Gang* books every year."

"Three a year plus a *Super Special*, to be exact. They're not my stories. I don't write them."

"What?" I puzzled.

"The publisher hires people to do it. The editors think up the plots and get somebody else to write it."

"But your name is on the cover."

"That's because the kids know who I am. The publisher pays me for the use of my name."

"What about the *Boy Scout Buddies?*" I asked.

"I haven't written the last three. Believe it or not, they're written by a school teacher who lives someplace in Canada."

I was stunned. "How come you didn't tell me this before, Dad?"

"I'm not exactly proud of it. I've just run out of stories to tell. You disappointed in me?"

"Those stories with your name on the cover are written by somebody else? How could you let someone do that?"

Dad smiled weakly. "The money's good."

"I was so proud of you every time there was a new book in the book club," I told him. "But it wasn't you at all, just a guy in Canada?"

"Don't sound like that, Robert. I didn't murder anybody. I just let them use my name. I worked hard in the beginning. I wrote all the early novels. I thought up the *Junior Romance Novels for Boys.*"

"Do you still write those?"

He shook his head. "Not anymore."

"Well, at least if I live with you I won't disturb your writing," I snarled. "I can't believe you'd really do something like this. It's like you sold out or something. You're using people."

"Don't start preaching to me," Dad said angrily. "Didn't you tell me you'd joined the track team so you wouldn't get booted out of school?"

"It's not the same. Putting your name on those books is lying."

"And when you fake a sprained ankle, that's not lying?" Dad said.

What could I say to that?

* * *

We didn't talk about anything else in the restaurant. And we didn't say much else on the drive back to Glowing

Embers. I was too scared and Dad was concentrating really hard on staying on his side of the road. Fortunately, nothing happened, but I was worried some cop would stop us for some reason and ask how much he'd had to drink.

"You wanna stay with me tonight?" Dad asked as we pulled into the campground.

"I guess."

He stopped at the convenience store and phoned Mom to tell her I was going to spend the night with him. He also bought another six-pack of beer, which he polished off while we watched a TV movie. By midnight, he was having trouble staying awake.

"Why don't you go to bed," I suggested.

"You still mad at me?"

"No."

"You're kinda quiet."

"I don't know what to say."

Dad's words came out all slurry. "Maybe I will hit the sack. I am tired. You pull the couch out when you're ready. The sheets are in the drawer."

He stumbled to his tiny bedroom and closed the door. I heard him going to the bathroom. Minutes later, he was snoring.

I fixed up my bed and lay in the darkness, completely confused. I'd thought as soon as Dad arrived, everything would be all right. I figured just talking to him would make school and Mom and the hassles go away.

I was wrong. Things were getting crazier than ever.

11

THE MOON IN JUNE

I listened to Dad's steady snoring and tried to fall asleep. It was no use.

"When in pain and doubt," I whispered into the darkness, "think of Rachel Parsons."

* * *

"There's no need to worry where you're going to sleep," I tell her. "You can sleep on the bed."

"But where will you sleep?" she asks.

"I, er . . . I, er . . . I have to stay awake and guard the door. We don't know what other terrible dangers lurk outside, especially when darkness falls."

"Oh Roob, you're so brave. I'm so lucky to be stranded on this deserted, tropical island with you. You're my knight in shining armor."

"I'm wearing leaves," I point out. "And you don't talk that way."

"What way?" she wonders.

"The way you've been talking in my imagination," I tell her. "I heard you at the track and in my Dad's truck. You don't talk silly. You talk normal."

"Normal?"

"Oh, it's nice. But it's normal."

"Sorry," she apologizes. "But this is your daydream. You're the one who is putting the words in my mouth."

"I know."

She takes my hand. "It's your father, isn't it?"

I nod. "My dad is an alcoholic. He just drinks and wanders around the country. He doesn't even write his own books anymore. That's kind of like being a bum. A wealthy bum. But still a bum. I'm going to go for a walk."

"But what about that horrible dinosaur thing, Roob?"

"I'll make it go away. I created it and I can make it disappear."

"Can you make me disappear too?"

"Sure," I answer.

Rachel fizzles out of sight like she's been beamed up to the *U.S.S. Enterprise*.

* * *

It must have been close to dawn by the time I fell asleep. Because I hadn't slept much the night before either, I ended up sleeping past noon. When I woke up, I was alone.

Dad had left a note on the fridge. "Gone to visit the Bakers, the couple from Nevada. "Won't be long."

I found some cereal and milk and watched some preacher on TV. I wondered if Mom had cooled off yet. For some reason, I felt the need to talk to her, even though I didn't know what I wanted to say.

I still couldn't get over the fact Dad didn't write his own books anymore. Wasn't it a matter of pride?

And his drinking. He may only drink beer and wine, but he sure packed away a lot of booze last night. Was that all he did with his life, tool around in his 4x4 and trailer and drink beer? What kind of life was that?

But what hurt most were the lies. He'd promised me he'd stopped. He'd lied to me.

"I hate those shows," Dad said as he opened the trailer door. "That guy will be found gambling in a few months."

He had another six-pack in his hand, and even from across the trailer, I could smell he'd already been drinking. "Those TV evangelists are all frauds."

"Some of them aren't," I said.

He sat at the table, opened a can and finished it off in two swallows. "I see you found the Corn Flakes. I didn't want to wake you. You looked like you were dreaming about that Rachel girl. I had to go say good-bye to the Bakers before they left. They're sorry they missed you. They're a funny couple."

"I guess everything seems funny after a couple of drinks."

I watched Dad's knuckles whiten as he squeezed the beer can. The aluminum crinkled, sounding like nails on a chalkboard. "Give it a rest," he ordered. "You're starting to bother me."

"Sorry," I said, even though I wasn't.

Dad pitched the can and opened another. "Now, this crazy idea you have about living with me, I've thought about it and the answer is no. You wouldn't fit into my life."

"How come I fit when you were married to Mom? I was a part of your life until I was eight years old. What's the difference now?"

"The difference is I've seen the light. Remember what I told you? Everything you do will seem stupid in a few years. Being married to your mom and having you and Helen seems stupid to me now."

"Boy, that really makes me feel good."

Dad closed his eyes and rubbed his forehead for a moment. "Okay, that came out wrong. I don't regret it. I don't regret having you as my son. I'm real proud of you, Robert. It's just that I'm older now. More mature. I see the mistakes I made. I don't want to repeat them."

"I don't understand."

"Of course not. You're just a kid. You've got to go through stuff."

"And after I go through stuff, do I end up like you?"

He smiled and saluted with his beer can. "You bet, cool and crazy."

"You know, Dad, yesterday at this time, being like you was exactly what I wanted to be like when I grew up. Isn't it amazing how fast someone can change their mind?"

"Don't get like the guy on the TV. This is life, son. You do what you do."

"And what you do is drink."

"I don't have to take your insults!" he shouted.

"It's not an insult. It's just the truth."

"Then maybe now is a good time to drive you back to your mother."

"Yeah, I want to go home, but you're not going to drive me. I should have said something last night. I'm not driving with you while you're drinking."

"Damn! Enough already!"

"It's stupid, Dad. Just plain stupid. You're going to end up dead. Or worse, you're going to kill somebody else."

He tossed the second can and popped a third. "So start walking."

I put my bowl in the sink, rinsed it and grabbed my jacket. I left Dad's trailer and for the third time in as many days I had to wipe tears off my cheeks.

* * *

I figured it would take me over an hour to walk home along Grand Boulevard. I didn't want to think about Dad, so I thought about Rachel Parsons.

It was no good picturing her on the island. I'd never be able to get that daydream back. So I thought about Rachel as the Maid of the Mist. There's a legend told to tourists about the Indians who lived around the Falls many years ago. It tells the story of a beautiful Native girl who paddled her canoe over the Falls to stop the anger of a terrible thunder god who lived in the rocks below.

* * *

I picture Rachel Parsons, dressed in buckskin, hair pleated, wearing a headband, stepping into a birchbark canoe.

The members of her tribe line the banks of the Niagara River.

The proud chief steps forward. "Rachel," he says. "Rachel-with-the-Twinkles-on-Her-Teeth, you have been chosen because you are the most beautiful girl in our tribe."

Rachel bats her eyelashes. "I know."

"You know our custom," the chief continues. "We must sacrifice our most beautiful maiden to the thunder god who lives at the bottom of the Falls."

"I know," Rachel smiles. "I go to my death happy to serve my people."

Her tribe breaks into a cheer.

"Does anybody want fries before I leave?" Rachel asks.

The chief pushes the canoe into the roaring current and Rachel is whipped toward the abyss.

Her canoe rocks and bobs in the river. Rachel's braids flow behind her.

Just as the canoe is about to tip over the edge, everything stops, frozen in time. Rachel looks angry.

"You know," she says. "First the Albertosi . . . Albertosi . . . Albertoso . . . the dinosaur thing and now plunging over Niagara Falls. I'm getting tired of his garbage, Roob."

Suddenly, I'm in the canoe with her, peering down the brink of the world's most impressive waterfall.

"Sorry," I tell her. "It keeps me from thinking about my

problems. You know. School. Mom. Paul. And now Dad. What am I going to do, Rachel?"

"The moon in June is a big balloon."

"Huh? Why'd you say something so silly?"

"You're making up my words, Roob," she points out. "You said something silly because you don't have any answers."

"Right."

* * *

A car honked and a blue Cavalier pulled up to the curb. It was Paul's mom.

"Need a ride?" she asked.

"You bet. Thanks." It was getting downright convenient to have the Lawson family as my chauffeur.

After I'd climbed in and she pulled back into traffic, she asked. "What are you doing way out here?"

"Walking home. I spent last night with Dad at the campground."

"Paul told us your dad showed up at practice yesterday. You left early to spend time with him. You must be very happy to see each other."

"At first, but it went a little sour. We had a disagreement about something. That's why I'm walking home."

"Oh." Paul's mom didn't press for the details. "I'm sorry I was so snippy with you at school on Friday. You know, about Paul and Mr. Lawson. It's just that things have been so tense around home. Mr. Lawson has high expectations now that Paul is almost finished middle school."

"Maybe eighth grade is the time boys and fathers don't see eye to eye, huh?" I suggested. "Maybe it's a year we don't get along."

"Perhaps," she said. "Paul and his father had a rough time last night. Apparently, after you left practice yesterday, the coach told Paul he was going to be a substitute."

"Oh, no," I said. "I bet Mr. L went snake city, right?"

"Let's say Mr. Lawson was upset. He told Paul he wasn't training hard enough."

"Paul's been busting his buns," I said.

"It was quite an argument. Paul was just about beside himself."

"How's Paul now?"

Mrs. Lawson broke into a wide grin. "Much, much better. In fact, Paul asked his Dad if he'd like to go for a walk today."

"A walk?" I stared at Mrs. Lawson.

"Paul said he wanted to talk to his father. He wanted to show him something. I hope they get to know each other again. I hope they find a way to stop fighting with each other."

"A walk?" A sickening feeling began to spread up my chest.

"Yes," she said. "I dropped them off an hour and a half ago. Then I went into Buffalo to get some fabric. We'll pick them up on the way home."

I sucked in my breath. There's no way it's what you're thinking. Stay calm, Roob, I told myself. You've got a weird imagination. Think of the dopey stuff you thought about with Rachel Parsons. This is the same thing, just your imagination.

"Where did they go for a walk?" I asked, trying to keep the panic from my voice.

"Goat Island," she answered. "That's one of Paul's favorite spots. You two went there Friday night, didn't you?"

"Oh my God," my voice came out dry and squeaky.

At that moment I discovered Mom was right when she once said, "Mothers have a sixth sense. They know when their children are in trouble." If it was possible for Mrs. L to look the same color as me, she did at that moment. Her bottom lip trembled slightly. "Something is wrong, isn't it?"

12

A LONG SHOT

"What's wrong?" Mrs. Lawson wanted to know. "Why did you say 'Oh my God'?"

"It's probably nothing," I answered, trying to sound calm. "It's just . . . well . . . Paul did something stupid on Friday night and . . . it's probably only my imagination."

"What did he do?" Mrs. L demanded.

For a few seconds, I debated whether to tell her or not. I didn't want to scare her. What if Paul and his dad were on a walk to sort things out? If I snitched and revealed the stupid bridge stunt, he'd be in more trouble.

But I was scared. Scared silly. My hands were cold and the metal taste I'd had Friday crept back into my mouth. I remembered Paul's laughter and the weird look in his eyes. I knew he could do it again. He'd do exactly the same thing to scare his father, to get to his dad. So I told Mrs. Lawson what Paul had done.

She didn't say anything when I finished. She just sat, staring ahead at the road, driving the same speed.

"It's probably stupid to think he'd do it again with his dad," I said.

"They've been there an hour and a half," she whispered.

"I should have known something was wrong. I should have done something a long time ago."

"I'm sure everything is going to be fine. I'm just being stupid." Neither one of us believed that.

It took us a few minutes to reach the Falls. I flew out of the Cavalier as Mrs. Lawson was parking. I raced down the street toward the pedestrian bridge to Goat Island. I wasn't sure what I was rushing for, I just felt I should be doing something, and doing it in a hurry.

I suppose I should have felt shocked and scared when I got to the bridge and saw the awful scene. And I was. But, at the same time, I somehow expected to see it, almost like I was reading it in a book, like the plot had already been written and I was a character acting out my part.

What I saw was a replay of Friday night. Paul was on the other side of the railing, leaning out over the river. Only this time the audience was different. His dad stood in front of him, wearing an expression of horror and bewilderment. He looked as if the whole universe had suddenly turned inside out. Which when I think about it, is exactly what had happened to him.

Two policemen stood on either side of Mr. Lawson, a couple of meters away, holding back the dozen or so tourists who had stopped to watch. I pushed my way to the front. I rammed my elbow into a man filming the horrible scene on his camcorder.

The burly, gray-haired policeman thrust out a straight arm to stop me from getting closer.

"Paul!" I shouted.

Paul looked at me. "Let him past," he ordered. "Let him past or else I let go."

The policeman didn't lower his arm. "Come on, son," he said. "We're here to help you. Climb back over and we'll talk about all the things bothering you."

Paul raised his left arm in the air. "Now!" he shouted.

"Don't be silly, son," the cop soothed as he lowered his arm. I rushed over to Paul.

"Stop!" Paul ordered, grabbing the rail with both arms again. "Don't come any closer, Roob. You're not going to trick me."

I swallowed, trying to make spit so I could talk. "I'm not going to trick you. I'm your friend, man."

"Right." Paul's arms were shaking, as if he was getting tired. "Just like you were my friend yesterday at the track practice? Didn't you say you were going to sprain your ankle? Well, you ran so fast I was made sub."

"Rachel was there," I told him. "I had to show off. You know how it is with me and Rachel."

He nodded. "I still don't want you coming any closer."

"Why can't I wake up?" Mr. Lawson whimpered like a little kid. "Why won't this bad dream go away? Please help me, Robert."

"Come on, kid," the other cop shouted. "Climb back over and we promise we'll listen to you."

"Yeah, Paul," I echoed. "Climb back and we'll talk."

"Look at his face, Roob," Paul said. "Look at my father's face. He can't believe it. He can't believe I'm doing this. His good boy who gets the good grades. His good boy who trained so hard to make the dumb track team so his father would get off his back. He can't believe I'm doing this."

"I'm so sorry," Mr. Lawson pleaded.

"You should have seen him, Roob. At first, he *ordered* me to climb back. He couldn't believe it when I wouldn't. He went to grab me and I . . ." He waved his arm again.

Mr. Lawson stared at Paul. "I'm so sorry," he repeated.

"Use both hands. Please," I begged.

Paul did what I asked.

I heard Mrs. L calling something from the crowd, pleading, whimpering. Paul glanced in her direction.

"You're hurting other people besides your dad," I

pointed out. "Think of what your mom is going through right now. And do you know what you're doing to me? I'm scared spitless."

He took a deep breath and slumped, making the crowd release a collective gasp. I blew out my breath.

"You did what you wanted, Paul," I said. "You upset everyone. When you talk, everyone is going to listen from now on."

"Your friend is right," the gray-haired cop called. "Let us help you."

Paul's face shone and he looked almost peaceful. Then he gave a tired smile. "All right, Roob, it's over. The last thing I want to do is die."

He raised his leg over the railing. At that moment, everything changed. The world seemed to slow down. It was like I was wearing 3-D glasses. Everything close up got super sharp. Everything in the distance fuzzed into a colored blur.

The burly cop dived at Paul. He was trying to grab him, to pull my friend to safety in case he slipped, to make sure he got on the bridge. But he startled Paul. Paul jerked in surprise and let go of the rail. The cop grabbed empty space. Paul fell, spread-out like a snow angel, wearing a mask of raw fear, into the Niagara River.

The water swallowed him for a moment and vomited him several meters from the bridge. Paul thrashed against the current, coughing, fighting the surging rush. But there was no way he could beat the force of the water. The river carried him downstream.

I heard Mr. Lawson cry in panic. Mrs. Lawson screamed. So did lots of people in the crowd. Maybe I did too.

I don't remember how I got through the crowd. Later, the cop told me I charged through everyone like I was a defensive tackle. But somehow I melted through the people on the Goat Island side. I found myself running along the sidewalk toward the edge of the Falls.

No, running isn't the right word. I was high on adrenalin, flying on terror. It felt like my Pumps weren't even touching the ground. I flew through the air.

I was aware of Paul thrashing in the foam and swirls, trying to fight his way closer to shore. I knew he'd never make it. He'd run out of river first. I fought to keep the picture of Paul falling onto the rocks out of my mind.

"Keep it up! Try to swim closer!" I shouted to him.

I had a plan. It was the longshot of longshots. I had to do the impossible. I had to run faster than the river was carrying Paul. Then I had to be in the right place at exactly the right time. But it was the only chance my friend had.

I found myself strangely angry. Why had Paul done something so stupid? Why couldn't he and his dad have talked things out? Why was he going to die over a spot on a dumb track team?

I saw my target, the old red maple with the exposed roots angled out over the river. I had to make it there before Paul did.

I didn't think I could run any faster, but I tried. I reached deep down within and pushed out whatever reserves I had. I jumped onto the tree trunk, scrambled up and threw myself flat on the bark, letting my right arm dangle over the river.

"Grab my arm!" I yelled. "Grab my arm!"

Paul was being whipped and tossed by the current. I'll never forget his eyes at that moment. They were wide and white, darting about as if they were loose in his head, reflecting the brutal knowledge that in less than a minute he was going to die.

"Grab my arm!" I shouted again.

Above the roar and whoosh, he must have heard my holler because his eyes locked on me. Frantically he kicked and splashed trying to get closer to the shore.

The Falls were so close, their thunderous symphony

drowned the pounding of the rapids. The fine mist made rainbows dance above the water.

I hugged the tree with my left arm and dug my fingers into the rough grooves of the bark so I had a solid grip. I concentrated on Paul hurtling toward me. For a second I thought he was too far out, that he'd flash past out of my reach, but a churning eddy whipped him straight at me.

Paul had his right arm raised and was waving it around, unsure in the boiling water exactly where I was.

"It's up to you," I said to myself. "You're the one who has to make it work."

I reached forward as far as I could and grabbed for his hand.

"I'm going to do it," I said. "I'm going to . . ."

Almost! I timed it wrong. Paul was going so fast I missed his fingers. My hand flew through empty air . . .

. . . and grabbed the cuff of his jacket.

I clamped my fingers into the leather, forming a tight fist. Paul stopped with a vicious jerk that almost yanked my arm out of its socket and almost ripped me right off the trunk.

"Aaaah!" I cried as pain shot through my shoulder. I fought to hold onto both Paul and the tree.

The water raged around him. There was no way I could hold on. The current was too strong. My arm was a sleeve of pain. I forced my fingers to stay wrapped around the jacket cuff.

I closed my eyes, concentrating, imagining my fist was the only thing in the universe. I pressed my teeth into the bitter bark of the maple.

I was losing him. I felt my grip weakening. I'd saved my friend only to lose him.

Suddenly, I felt a heavy weight on my back and heard someone shouting into my ear. "Okay, kid, I got him."

When I opened my ears, I became conscious of the burly

cop, helped by his partner, edging back down the trunk, dragging Paul by the arm. A handful of tourists stood on the bank and helped pull my friend from the river.

"Don't move," the cop called to me. "Don't move until I come and get you."

I saw Paul's mom and dad burst through the crowd and rush over to him. They sat on the bank, crying and clutching each other.

"Okay, son." The cop had a hold of my leg. "I've got you. Take it easy."

I edged back slowly, watching the river rage beneath me. For some reason, it appeared colder and more violent than it had a minute ago, as if it was angry.

Once I was on the bank, the tourists surrounded me. Someone was patting me on the back and shouting into my ear. Another threw a coat around me. All of a sudden I was shaking like a leaf.

And why was someone crying? Who was crying so loud their sobbing filled my head? Why were they so close? As I slipped to my knees, I realized the sobs were my own.

13

PROMISES AND RACHEL

The next morning, I sat eating a second helping of French toast and sausages at the kitchen table. Mom doesn't usually make a big breakfast, but she'd gone out of her way to treat me like a prince ever since the police called her from the hospital yesterday afternoon.

My right arm was in a sling and sore as heck. The doctors said I'd stretched the ligaments in my elbow, that I'd need the sling for a week. But I could put up with the pain, considering everything turned out fine.

"I still can't believe you saved Paul's life," Mom said as she loaded the dishwasher.

"That's about the hundredth time you've said that," I pointed out.

"It's still an amazing thing, Robert. Just think what would have happened if you weren't there. Nobody else knew about the maple tree. And probably no one could run as fast as you did."

"I wish you'd stop talking about it all the time. It's kind of embarrassing."

"Enjoy it," Mom told me. "It's not every day you get to be a hero."

"Maybe it wouldn't have happened if I'd told you what Paul did on Friday night."

"We talked about that last night, Roob," Mom said. "Stop feeling guilty about it. You did what you thought was right. Even though you were wrong, you were still thinking about your friend. If something like this ever happens again, you'll know what to do."

"Ever happens again? Once in a lifetime is too many times."

"Do you want some more French toast?"

"No thanks. Do you think you can drive me down to the hospital to visit Paul this evening?" I asked.

She smiled. "Definitely."

"How long do you think he'll have to stay there?"

"Hard to say," she answered. "They kept him overnight to make sure he didn't go into shock. I imagine they'll keep him a few more days to do some tests." She pointed at her forehead. "He'll have to talk to a psychiatrist. He did try to commit suicide."

"I don't believe that. Paul wasn't trying to kill himself. Like I told you, he was trying to scare his dad. Before he fell, he said the last thing he wanted was to die."

We both fell silent. I think Mom was thinking what was in my head. What would today have been like without Paul?

I took a swallow of orange juice. "You know, I was thinking last night in bed and I think I understand something about people that I didn't before."

"What's that?" Mom wondered.

"Well," I began, "it seems everyone has problems. You know, we all have something in our lives that doesn't work."

"People always have problems," Mom agreed. "That's part of life."

"Yeah," I went on. "But the trick is not to let the problem get to a point where it beats you. The trick is not to let it get out of hand. Paul and his dad let their problem get away from them."

"That's pretty obvious," Mom said.

"And Dad's drinking has got away from him. Unless he gets himself together . . ." My words trailed off. I didn't want to say out loud what I was thinking.

She sat down and smiled sympathetically. "I'm sorry you had to see the truth about your father."

"I knew it before," I told her. "When I was little and he was still living with us, I knew it. I knew it when he visited us each year. I just couldn't admit it until yesterday."

"Only he can help himself, Robert."

I nodded. "I know. I wonder if he'll call again before he drives on."

Mom shrugged her shoulders a little to tell me she didn't know. "Maybe. He hasn't seen Helen yet."

I wondered if seeing his daughter was all that important to him.

"I know what my problem is," I announced.

"And what is that?"

"I'm a jerk."

"What?" Mom laughed.

"I'm a jerk," I explained. "Oh, I'm a nice jerk, but I'm still a jerk. I fool around at school because I like to do it. I don't tidy my room because I'm lazy. I figure I better do something about my problem before I find myself neck deep."

Mom stared at me with a wry smile on her face. She obviously didn't believe me.

I smiled too. "I'll clean up my room because if I don't, you and I will just keep arguing and arguing. I don't want us to end up hating each other's guts."

"We'd never do that," Mom said.

"I'm sorry about the stuff I said on Saturday. I didn't mean it."

"And I'm sorry I lost my temper. I was just so frustrated. If you're willing to be cleaner, I guess I'll try to turn a blind eye once in a while."

"We can talk, Mom," I repeated. "Now about school, that's going to be tougher. But I'm going to try. Could you drop me off on your way to work?"

"I think you should rest today," Mom said. "You deserve a day off school."

I shook my head. "I've got track practice. Even if my arm is wrecked, I can still run to keep in shape. City meet is in two weeks. Besides I have a lunch date."

"A date?"

"With this girl. Her name is Rachel Parsons. You'll really like her."

Mom looked genuinely pleased. "You *are* growing up, aren't you?"

* * *

As soon as I walked into the lunchroom, I saw Rachel Parsons sitting by herself. She'd chosen the table at the far end of the room, the one nobody usually sat at. As soon as she saw me, she flashed her nearly perfect smile and waved.

Considering the fact that my best friend had almost been killed the day before and it was possible I could have been pulled off the tree and into the river, I figured nothing could scare me anymore.

Wrong.

The sight of Five Freckles on Her Nose filled me with agony. As I walked toward her, the floor turned to a rubber sheet under my feet.

"Hi, Roob." She grinned. "I sat here hoping you'd remember to eat lunch with me."

"Ta . . ." I croaked.

"Pardon me?"

I swallowed. "Thanks, I'd like to."

I slid into the chair, grateful to rest my wobbly legs.

"Everybody is talking about you," she said. "That was a wonderful thing you did yesterday. I wish I'd been there."

"It was nothing," I said as modestly as possible.

"Tell me about it."

"Maybe later, okay?"

She flashed more silver as her grin widened. "Sure. How's your arm?"

"It'll be better in a few days."

"That's good. How's your father? His new *Baby-Watchers* book is really good. He's a great writer."

"Dad is . . . Dad is Dad."

Rachel opened a magazine on the table. "You ever read *Fifteen*?" she asked.

I shook my head. "No, it's for girls."

"I guess it is. I've been doing this test in here. It's supposed to tell you how romantic you are. There's one question that asks, 'Who would you most like to spend time with on a deserted, tropical island?' Who do you think I picked?"

"Fred Savage?" I answered.

She laughed, so cute-like. "Of course not. I chose you."

"You did?"

She nodded. "I think being alone on an island would let us become close friends, like in *Blue Lagoon*. Did you ever see the movie?"

"No."

"Why don't we rent it and you can come over to my house and we'll watch it together."

"Okay."

"I've been wanting to talk to you like this ever since I came to Maid of the Mist," she confessed. "It wasn't just because of your father's books. I thought you were really cute the first time I saw you."

I knew I was blushing. "Na . . ." I cleared my throat. "No kidding."

"Did you notice me before we met on Saturday?" she wondered.

"Yeah, sort of."

"Did you ever want to talk to me?"

"Sort of."

She closed the magazine. "What do you think we'd do if we ever got stranded on a deserted island together."

"Well, we could, er . . ."

"Yes?"

"We could, um . . ."

"We could what, Roob?"

"We could wear leaves."

"Wear leaves?"

"And I could pick you a ripe, tasty coconut. And we could find Robinson Crusoe's abandoned cave. And hide from a dinosaur that time forgot."

She laughed again. "That's really creative. How did you think of it so fast?"

"I think I dreamt it once," I told her.

"It must have been an interesting dream."

"It was," I said. "But real life is better."

I pointed at the math test sticking out of her binder. "A-, huh? Great mark. Who's your math teacher?"

"Old Lady Dawson."

"She's mine too. Say, Rachel, I'm flunking math. Would you help me with it?"

Her faced seemed to shine. "I'd be delighted."

"And maybe history too?"

"That's my best subject."

"Then there's the project for the science fair."

"I'm almost finished mine," Rachel said. "It's a display of

Inter-flux Particles Caught in Cosmic Stasis with Polar Lateral Gravitational Fields."

"Huh?"

"Fun things to do with a magnet," she explained. "You could help me finish it. We can submit it together."

"Thanks a lot. I'm going to have to work real hard in the next couple of months to make my year. I can use all the help I can get. I don't want to have to spend another year at Maid of the Mist."

Her features formed an expression of sincere concern.

I grinned. "Hey, Rachel, don't worry about me. I'm just . . . Naw, I'm not crazy."